MOULT

MOULT

A novel in short stories

Andy Baird

ASHWOOD
PUBLISHING

ISBN-paperback: 978-1-7641254-4-4
ISBN-epub: 978-1-7641254-5-1

Published by Ashwood Publishing, Cradoc, Tasmania.
ashwoodpublishing.com.au
info@ashwoodpublishing.com.au

Stonehouse excerpts, translated by Red Pine, from
The Mountain Poems of Stonehouse. Copyright © 1986, 1999, 2009, 2014 by Red Pine. Reprinted with the permission of The Permissions Company, LLC on behalf of Copper Canyon Press, coppercanyonpress.org.

The Tibetan Book of the Dead (and of Great Liberation) quotes are from Sogyal Rinpoche's book *The Tibetan Book of Living and Dying*, 1993, Rigpa Fellowship, New Delhi.

The David Hansen quote in 'Moulting Lagoon' is from *John Glover and the Colonial Picturesque*, Tasmanian Museum & Art Gallery and Art Exhibitions Australia, Hobart, 2003.

The author gratefully acknowledges Aki Matsusa for her English translation of Bashō's famous haiku written in Japanese around 1691.

Cover: Susan Young. Buddha photo: Andy Baird.

The work of Ashwood Publishing is nurtured by the beautiful country of the Melukerdee people in the Huon Valley in southern Lutruwita/ Tasmania. We acknowledge and pay respect to the traditional owners and their continuing custodianship of this place.

A catalogue record for this work is available from the National Library of Australia

Contents

Under the Silence

1996

THERE WAS THE BRIEFEST FLICKER in his eyes when I touched
him. Little else this morning, just a tiny acknowledgement of
my presence. A trembling, of the lids really, a muscle twitch
of that frail skin tracked with blue veins. Acknowledgement
probably too strong a word. That's hope speaking, my need to
have a little more time with him. Yesterday there was at least
the glassy following of my movements around the bed as I disappeared behind nurses changing his sheets and wetting his lips.
Yesterday his watery eyes, though pale and opaque, did track
me – someone or something worth attending to more than the
staff who came and went without eliciting his response. It was
as if he'd been there so long he knew everything he needed to
know about all that. 'All that', which was keeping his body alive,
which *was* his body, but not him.

At least I'm hoping this is true, but now it's changed again and
even his eyes have become – what? Unseeing seems too banal.

Reticent, mute, inarticulate? Until now I'd hoped he still saw me somehow as not part of all this, but of something bigger, older… more important. Part of him, as all this materiality was not. All the *activity*: the bedpans clanging, the sharp purposeful footsteps, that bloody constant hum of air-conditioning. The oxygen line wiring him to the walls. The walls themselves. It was not how he should be seen, and I hated the way it took over, silencing him. But now, amidst the tiny expansiveness that opened with the retreat of the busyness, I'm left facing something simpler, yet huge and urgent, and wondering if it's all too late, if he's already left. Wondering who he is now. Was. Is?

Because I still don't know what happened, at the house, on the property, back in '69.

A sunken face, pulled inwards by gravity, stares out at me. Mouth agape, the features narrowed and the flesh shrivelling by the moment, my father's face has become a stranger's. Ghoulish, without the horror, just the otherworldliness of the dying – a face belonging to a country called 'dying'. The skull's presence is overtaking as if breaking through the skin, the form transcending the function. Already it's becoming a body not a being. Already the life force is leaking away, leaching away like some great personal epoch of weathering: the rubbing out of life.

I can't even tell when he's asleep anymore. His cloudy eyes don't focus; his eyelids open and fall at random. I remember him falling asleep for real once, at the wheel, and I can still taste the fear as my mother shouted at him, reaching across me to shake him awake. Punched him. He woke with a start, braked, overcorrected and Bess our EH Holden spun wildly on the gravel, fishtailing and throwing up great clouds of dust and rock, our screams ricocheting off each other. Somehow, he regained control and pulled up on the empty road, and we all just sat shaking, listening to the sounds of the gorge out over the edge. That deep silent sound of our valley from up high where the emptiness echoes. I recall wondering how he could have fallen asleep on our swerve-curvy road. Mum was rigid with shock and rage and stared straight ahead (perhaps into a future of mangled children?). Gripping the wheel with big hairy hands, he looked ahead through the dust that was swirling off over the void and said nothing. I don't remember where we'd been driving home from, some holiday I guess, but I do remember the sound of pied currawongs filling the emptiness, ringing in that exhausted suspense after the adrenaline rush, and finally my brother cracking a nervous joke about a nice place for a picnic. He was good like that, Bill. He knew when to let go, most of the time.

Me, I haven't been able to fall asleep in a car since, driving or not.

My father used to love the silence (silence without drama, that is). Held it sacred, even in his speech, which was slow and peppered with pauses. He used to sit out on the porch, look out over the forest in the late afternoon and just listen. Dwelling in a quietude made profound by the gentlest of winds and the reverberations of an occasional bird call. Those currawongs, or the yellow-tailed black cockatoos who'd descend off the mountain when the rains threatened, an echoing refrain of *wee-lah, wee-lah* that laced the steep-sided valley and somehow gave space to the air, to the emptiness, that was everything other than their calls. They announced the void. He always resisted the trend to the coast because, he used to say, the sea was too noisy. All that pounding, roaring, even the backwash on the calmest day, was too much. Not enough long pauses. Not enough gaps. Too full. I understand that too, now.

He really would have preferred to dwell in silence all the time, but with a family of three boys he didn't get much opportunity. We would notice sometimes, when all our yelling and carrying on had run out of steam for a moment, that he had gone, and we would find him later up the track at the 'Bus Stop', sitting, listening, watching out over the gums, tracking sounds with his eyes. We named it the Bus Stop – the old, flaking green wooden bench he had lugged through the bush to a flat sandstone out-crop – after we found him there once and asked what he was doing. 'Waiting for a bus,' he replied.

Later, when we had all gone one way or another, including Mum, he still used to sit there with his cane resting against a leg. I asked him once why he bothered, with the house empty, the porch quiet and the tangled track a trip hazard. He replied that the sound was different up there, more resonant, deeper, cleaner. After a long delay, he added, 'And habits hold fast.'

Since the nursing home move and now here in the hospice, I haven't been game enough to mention the silence – or the noise – and he hasn't said anything. I should have asked him about that. It worries me that he can't get away from noise here, can't hear the silence. Does it worry him?

—

I don't know what to do here now, in this waiting, wondering if I've missed the boat. I watch the monitors, the read-out of his oxygen levels; watch his heartbeat as an electronic trace.

Occasionally, I shift my hand that holds his, careful with the tubes that are attached through hairless, bruised, mottled skin. A shrunken hand, a contracting life.

⁓

My thoughts keep drifting back to that night in '69 when we were last all together. It's a memory replayed with a regularity that has trapped me, grooved me, scarred me. Back to a home on the New England tablelands and all that noise, the yells and screams, the shattering glass and hurled plates. Slamming doors.

It was one of the only times in that crowded house with its thin, rough-clad walls and tacked-on bedrooms that he'd stayed in the house when the shouting started, and I still wish he hadn't. I wish he'd got on the bloody bus.

It started out sedately enough, just Bill, Mum and Dad sitting around the dining table, reading the letter Bill had been holding all afternoon since he'd come back with the post from town. I was twelve years old, lying on the sofa, drawing, immersed in some childhood creation, but I could feel something was up and had shaded in the same spot on the page till it was a dark black splotch. I'd seen the letterhead, the coat of arms, the 'Department of Labour and National Service' printed below, and Bill had been jittery and tense all afternoon.

When Dad finally spoke, he took off his glasses and looked sternly at Bill.

'You have to go, son.'

The air was still with expectation, dust and smoke from the wood-stove hanging.

'It's not my war. It's bollocks,' Bill said with frustration, and the thin leash that had held back his afternoon's torment began to rip. Bill was not the fighter in the family, and avoided conflict whenever he could. The middle child, though considerably older than me, he was the patient one, the helper in the wings, gracefully entering and exiting the family squabbles waving the white flag of truce. While the rest of us blazed, Bill skilfully sidestepped, but often, I suspect, he smouldered. And this time the wind was definitely fanning the fire.

'It's all our war son, no different to the others.'

My father's conservatism was long evident, and although he was a builder from working-class origins, he'd grown his small business on a model of self-help that he aligned with Menzies-style liberalism. For the most part he was unreflective on this conservatism. Politics held no great sway in his life and he implicitly trusted the country's leadership to 'do the right thing'. He saw no problem with Harold Holt's proclamation that Australia should go 'all the way with LBJ'.

Bill, on the other hand, was an avid politics watcher, and many a night across our shared bedroom, I'd see him glued to the transistor radio, listening intently.

'But it is. It's fucked. We shouldn't be there.'

'We're there, and now it's your turn to stand up for your county,' Dad said.

'This isn't about 'my country'. It's about fucking America and reds under the bed, and, and ... it's crap!'

Bill was shaking.

'Watch your mouth around your mother,' Dad said, still measured in the face of Bill's rage, but with a hint of displeasure creeping in at his son's disregard.

'Shh, Frank, it's OK,' said Mum, trying to placate as always.

'No, it's not OK, Mum,' Bill yelled, throwing back his chair with a crash and rising to his feet. 'He's getting on his high horse because he's still feeling guilty about not signing up thirty fucking years ago, even though he was making guns or shit, and THAT'S GOT NOTHING TO DO WITH ME!'

He was tall, my brother, six-foot-two and built like the proverbial, but usually gentle as a lamb. Panda, I'd call him. I could pester him for hours and he wouldn't react, but this time he was red in the face and angry.

Dad looked up at him coldly, his voice steely flat.

'You have no choice Bill, it's the lottery,' he said.

'I do have a choice. I can piss off down south or I could just tell them I ain't gunna fight.'

'My son will not be a dodger, I won't allow it.'

Dad was now fired up too and he used his authority like a hammer, crashing down on Bill's remarks. When he broke his silence and spoke, the household was expected to listen. He didn't like it when things went awry.

'It isn't your choice, Dad. It's mine, and I can do what I fucking like,' Bill yelled.

The door swung open and our other brother was standing there.

'What's going on?'

Mick dumped his toolbelt in the corner and looked at the two of them. Mum shook her head in warning, but as usual he ignored it.

'What are you pissed off about, squirt?'

Mick thought he was the next in charge after Dad. Only a year older than Bill, shorter, fatter (musclier, he'd call it), he used to strut about trying to impress the old man whenever he could. Bill usually ignored it, but this time he was over it.

'Fuck off, Mick. It's none of your business.'

He kept his voice even but there was a clear warning tone.

'It *is* his business. You're his brother and you're signing up,' Dad said, handing the letter to Mick.

Mick read it slowly, his mouth silently moving till he read the last bit aloud.

'... in accordance with the provision of the National Service Act, to submit yourself to medical examination before a medical board ...'

He looked up at Bill.

'What's up little Willy? Scared they'll find you don't have a dick?'

If anyone else had said this, it would have been funny, yet Mick had a way of making something funny seem snide, always a put-down. And men were losing more than their dicks in Vietnam.

Bill snapped, grabbed a plate of biscuits and hurled it at him, following with a wild punch. But Mick, as well as being a prick, could box. He used to train with Dad's old gloves, spending hours in the shed, beating the crap out of some sacking hanging from the rafters. Dorrigo middleweight champion three years running. Mick ducked the plate that smashed through the door glass behind him, blocked Bill's flailing fist and returned hard with his own punch to the jaw.

'Fucking sissy. Too scared of the gooks are ya?' he taunted. Getting into a boxing stance and enjoying his show, Mick flicked his eyes towards Dad, seeking approval to go in hard.

'Enough, Mick. Bill, enough!'

Mum came around from the table and pushed her way between them. Dad just sat there watching, and then delivered the killer punch himself.

'I'll tell them where to find you, Bill. Be a man.'

I remember the shock on Bill's face, the look of betrayal, of someone suddenly cast adrift. And too, the memory of picking up one of the biscuits that had rolled and slid my way. ANZAC biscuits. It must have been one of the last I've ever eaten. I think Mum stopped baking them, they weren't just a biscuit after that.

—

Bill stormed out, feet crunching on broken glass. And yes, he did sign up and go off to the war. Mum told me years later that the day after this barney, Bill and Dad had talked for a long time while I was at school, both of them sitting up at the Bus Stop well into the cold night. She remembered worrying about them as the evening darkened, listening intently through the open kitchen window, the forest silent but for the boobook owls. She particularly remembered that, the sound of owl calls.

We got a few letters from camp and from Vietnam over the next eight months. He wasn't happy, unsurprisingly. When I read his letters now they reveal much more than what he wrote. How the glow of burning jungles populated his dreams and the smell of napalm made him sick. How he didn't think he'd be able to love summer at home anymore. Fires were no longer a fact of life, scary but blameless, but had become a weapon, with horrifying intent. There was nothing natural about the fires over there.

And then the news came that he'd lost both legs from a booby trap. An IED they would call it these days. They got him back to base alive, but he was too badly injured, he bled too much from his severed limbs. When I found out I sat in our bedroom and cried for days. My legless brother who'd once wanted to be a dancer but had grown too tall, now blown in half and coming home in a box. I cried and I raged, a twelve-year-old's fury at the injustice of it all, looking for blame and searing my family with accusations. But I never found out what my father said to make him go. Never felt my father's grief, never understood Bill's shouted references to the Second World War. Never knew if my father felt the guilt I was so keen he should. Never forgave him.

—

In the years that followed I marched in the moratoriums, a precocious and righteous teenager burning with pain, a firebrand fifteen-year-old reading *Das Capital* from the school library. Eventually I left the Tablelands for university in the city. My father couldn't understand why I didn't want to join him and Mick in the business, said he'd been looking forward to the '& Sons' being painted on the work ute, but I think he was happy to let me go. Perhaps he was tired of my rebellion. I sent him photos of various marches and demos in the following years – to piss him off I guess, and to keep reminding him.

As the decades passed we almost lost contact. I tried to forge a life away from the family back up there on the Tablelands, away from the memories. It didn't work out that well. I stayed away so long I couldn't return, wandered a lot and made a dead man my only family, leaving the living ones to decay. It took my mother's death and my father's decline to change the pattern, though it seems some things have become too entrenched.

Dad rarely spoke about Bill, and never mentioned that war, or any war really. I tried once, in more recent years, sitting with him in the nursing home with the Gulf War blazing away on the TV news, a few of the other residents reminiscing about how things had changed since their war service. I tried to ask him about what he did during that earlier war, but he refused to talk. A muteness in the silence.

⁓

And now I wonder if it is all too late. I've searched for the right moment these last few weeks, wondered how to start the story after so many years, and wondered too why I need to know. In this hospice room with its sanitised, distant views of treetops through a small, double-glazed window, facing west, away from the sea, towards the mountains. Mick thought I was mad demanding Dad get the window bed, but I think he was just jealous I'd thought to ask, not him – both of us imaginatively going back to that seat in the bush, but whether Dad did, who knows. During the first week here, Dad asked for some of his old photos to be placed around him, and rummaging in his single wardrobe in his old private room, I found one of all of us from the year Bill graduated – Dorrigo High, 1967. Dad and his three sons lined up on the porch. Mum must have taken it. Mick's already trying to look proprietorial over the place, arm up on the white gum posts he helped fell and strip of bark, standing next to Dad. Bill on the other side of the post with me, his school uniform a bit worse for wear. I'm the only one smiling. Seems I was happy then.

—

'Mr Ferguson, you're wanted on the phone.'

Breaking my reverie I look up at the nurse, and then look at Dad lying unresponsive, then back to her. Mr Ferguson?

'Your brother's on the line. It's over at the nursing station.'

Standing, I let go of Dad's hand and follow her to the phone. Mick was meant to take over from me on our vigil, but is delayed. Little Frankie's sick, his daughter Haley's playing up. I can't stay either – though work, not family, beckons. So I return to Dad's bedside and squeeze his hand goodnight. His eyes are closed and there's no response, just his chest slowly rising and falling. The machines pulse along.

What is it about the flesh that feels so solid and yet so ephemeral and fleeting at the same time? Flesh to which we cling so firmly. I cling. Dad, I don't know. Dad just fades away and yet, is still here. This body of his holding so many untold stories, the weathered lines on his face furrowed by experiences I cannot know. I have watched him these last few weeks, up close, unobserved, and seen a man I know so little about. A father I have presumed. Each day his skin has wrinkled a bit more, desiccating, folding like geological strata. Thin patchy hair, scabs on his scalp where he's picked, the blotched skin and wasted muscles. The forces of his life that have shaped the lines and weathered his body's terrain, I see them and him like I haven't for so many years. And still I don't know him. The gaps in the middle, and before, are too big.

—

An hour later the hospice calls to say he's died. He'd woken up, more alert than he had been for many a day and asked for the photo. The nurse said when he passed away he was holding it on his lap, his finger pointing to one of the boys, but she couldn't recall which one.

Night Travails

1997

'For fuck's sake Haley, you're not going out in that!'

Haley just looked at him, deadpan, hip thrust out, arms crossed, eyes glazed. A well-practised look.

'Grow a brain, girl! What do you think's gunna happen when you walk down the street dressed like a – like a – fuck I dunno what you're dressed like. Every bogan under the sun will be leering at you!'

Mick was flushed, a hot, flickering flame spreading up from his chest. A minute ago he'd been sitting on the recliner, aimlessly leafing through the newspaper, and now this. He'd already nearly lost it. A sense of inevitability washed over him, another train wreck on the way. Why the fuck couldn't she see what she's doing, why the fuck wouldn't she listen to him, why the fuck was he always the bad guy, the dumb fuck dinosaur. She was so bloody stupid. And so, so fucking rude!

Mick took in his daughter, again. She was beautiful, and yet turning into a mall rat. Smart, but smart-arsed in her every response. Clever, yet acted like a four-year-old. And treated him like a dick. Why was she turning out like this? He loved her more than he'd thought possible, and the pain in his chest was burning him up. He took a deep breath and tried to calm his rage, keep his voice level.

Was this what girls wore these days? Should wear? What would he know, he'd only grown up with brothers. Understanding her moods was like trying to understand a foreign language, just bloody chaos, a cacophony of crap. Same thing with Michelle, her passivity driving him spare, incessantly complaining about Haley's behaviour but never willing to do anything about it. Sniping from the side, but not wanting to get her hands dirty. It was always left to him to pull Haley into line. He was at his wits' end fighting this losing battle.

'You're not wearing that get-up. Go to your room and put something reasonable on.'

'I'm not twelve, Dad. You know fuck all about fashion.'

'That isn't *fashion*, Haley, that's *fucked*, which is where you'll end up.'

The words slipped out and he regretted them as soon as he said them. Haley left with a calculated flick of her dyed blond hair (she already *was* blond for god's sake!) and stormed off to her room, door slamming.

—

Haley sat on her old toy box, sniffling as tears streaked black down her face. Why didn't he get it? What was so wrong with what she was wearing? It wasn't any shorter than Jordan's at the party last Saturday, and Dad hadn't said anything when he dropped them both off that time. She knew she was putting it out there a bit, that was the point. But it wasn't like she was starkers, duh! The black miniskirt was short, the knee-high lace-up boots scarily stilettoed, the lipstick a neon red, and her new killer choker with fake diamond studs was, she felt, fuck'n awesome. Not particularly original, but the other girls would go wild that she could get away with it. And when she stripped out of the cut-off leather jacket and they saw the tatt, dude, they'd be super jealous! It was the shining glory of her new outfit. Keeping it covered had been tricky these last couple of weeks, and her dad would go ballistic if he knew she'd done it, but so what. At sixteen she knew how to handle him, and anyway, it *proved* she looked eighteen.

Her tears dried. She'd do what she liked. Stuff him.

Haley stood and looked at herself in the mirror, ignoring the disaster that was now her make-up. She shrugged her jacket off one shoulder, turning to get a glimpse of the new tattoo. The simple Om on a lotus bed was small but stark on her pale thin shoulder blade. She had wanted Kali, the goddess of destruction, and had sketched a magnificent multitude of flailing blue arms, imagining them curling up from behind her back and pointing a flaming trident down her arm. But the tattoo man had said a price that was way out of her league, not to mention the pain. Still, the Om was definitely cool. Once her dad got over the fact that she'd done it (okay, lying about her age might be another drama), she reckoned he would be into it. He was always banging on about his days travelling in Bali, regaling her with stories of all the mysticism and magic, the zillions of gods and goddesses, and she had begun to take interest in recent years, though she hadn't let on.

There was a knock at her door, and her mother called her.

'What?'

Haley kept her voice a monotone through the closed door as she pulled up the jacket. Here we go again, she thought, rolling her eyes and predicting the lecture: be responsible, think about the family, don't be rude to your father, blah blah blah.

'We need to talk, Haley. Your father's gone to the garage.'

'So, I don't need him to tell me what to wear. It isn't fair. I'm not changing.'

'Just open the door and let me in.'

'Forget it, Mum. I won't go then. I'll be the nun he wants me to be.'

'Haley. He's not saying you can't go and be who you are, or enjoy yourself. He's just worried.'

'I can look after myself. He's always mollycoddling me. Just leave me alone.'

'Well come out when you've made a bit of effort and we'll decide if you can go.'

Haley mumbled something in reply, but it was lost through the door and Michelle turned away in exasperation. It was always up to her to patch things up between those two, her job to keep the peace. They were so alike, so stubborn, so quick to flare up. She returned to the sofa and sat next to Frankie, cuddling up to him. At least he was easy to deal with, though god knew what would happen when he got to Haley's age. Frankie was only five, and a bit of a surprise since she and Mick had rarely shared a bed in those years. There was a period in their relationship, after the saga with *that* woman, when 'relationship' was a very tenuous word and they cohabited more than lived together. Occasionally, desperately, they'd make love in an attempt to shelter from each other's isolation, only to fall away again into their old habits. But Frankie had turned out to be her blessing, and though he was a frail child and a bit slow, he was her refuge on many a cold night. And warm ones, like tonight with the cicadas singing loudly, though he squirmed away from her now on the sticky leather cushions.

'Can I go for a swim, Ma?' Frankie asked, looking sideways out the living room window to the cool blue of the pool.

'Oh petal, I've just sat down and I'm too hot to move, and you know I can't let you swim alone. Anyway, it'll be dark soon.'

Frankie sulked and moved to the other end of the sofa, away from his mother. She sighed in exhaustion.

—

Michelle and Frankie watched TV for a while and were soon lost in the drama of car chases, doors slamming, engines revving, explosions and ads for discount furniture stores. After twenty minutes Mick came into the room and asked Michelle where Haley was.

'In her room, sulking.'

'Do you think that get-up was reasonable?'

Mick's voice was dull, masking his frustration.

'No, but I don't think swearing at her will change her mind.'

'Swearing at her? For god's sake, that's the least of our worries. She's dressed like a tart and you're worried about my language?'

Michelle looked up at Mick from over the back of the sofa and pointed silently at Frankie sitting next to her.

'Let's talk about this next door,' she said.

—

As they walked into the kitchen Michelle's thoughts turned to how it all used to be, and she felt her sadness rising. Mick and Michelle had been high school sweethearts, 'M & M' they'd been called by their friends and teased for their sweetness to each other. A fixture of coupledom by the time she finished matric., they'd rarely argued in those courtship days, avoiding disagreements by letting love and lust wash out the inevitable daily differences before they accumulated into anything noticeable. They talked endlessly about everything and could be seen sharing lunchtimes, huddled in conversation, holding hands on the grass behind the milk bar. Mick had been a real confidante for her and his sureness and sense of purpose was appealing, yet without the arrogance she saw in the other boys. After they were married they'd head up to bed each night and undress each other under the glow of the traffic light, the play of red, orange and green making their own theatre lighting. The sounds of cars and late-night revellers outside their tiny rented flat above the shoe shop masked their passionate cries. She so desperately missed all that – the intimacy of the closeness, a friend to talk to, to share with. Love.

In the last few years so much had fallen away and in its place the heaviness of baggage weighed exhaustedly. Michelle wondered about so many things now, things that once looked so innocent. Even the memories of their lightest, happiest moments were washed with doubt. Or bile. Haley's naming had come up recently in a conversation at a rare dinner party. Mick stuck to the story that he liked the music of her namesake, though conceding that his father's story of conceiving Mick after a Bill Haley and the Comets concert was in the mix. Michelle joked, somewhat bitterly, it was all due to Mick's infatuation with Halle Berry the actress and the only music it was referencing was in his loins.

They rarely agreed nowadays and, though there was a level of tolerance on both parts, their marriage appeared to be about endurance more than anything. It felt like years since Mick had truly held her. The only passion that sparked their relationship now was in their arguments, frequently about Haley.

—

'So, what's your strategy for getting her to listen?' Mick demanded when they were out of Frankie's earshot.

'She's only sixteen. She doesn't know what she's doing,' Michelle responded, and Mick shook his head in frustration.

'What. Are we. Going. To. DO. About it?'

He spoke the words in a slow staccato, emphasising them with thrusting open hands.

'Don't treat me like an idiot,' Michelle said, glaring stonily. 'I don't know what we're going to do.'

'So you'll leave it up to me as usual, and then blame me when I get it wrong!'

'I'm not blaming anybody, I just don't think yelling at her is going to work. Why are you yelling at me? Perhaps we could—'

'Well at least it's stopped her getting raped!' Mick interrupted, his voice rising uncontrollably. 'I'm going to ground her if she doesn't change.'

With that he turned and stomped down the corridor to Haley's room with Michelle's parting 'Don't antagonise her' trailing after him.

—

Antagonise her! Fuck me, he thought, what about everybody antagonising me! Approaching fifty, Mick was finding the world an increasingly hostile place. Everything was going to shit. People used to come to him to solve their problems and he could! Turn crap into concrete and build on it, make it stand tall, worth something. Now he couldn't see the dream, or it was faded, gone stale, had been ripped off. Who knew what was coming, but the younger mob were all over it: hyped up, ambitious, way too fucking good and they made sure to tell you, egos bigger than a skyscraper. Heartless bastards the lot of them. What at thirty looked like a pathway in his career had turned out instead to be a maze, one of those tourist topiaries where the participants all looked ridiculous when viewed from a slight rise. The light on the hill turned out to be the mocking glow from the members' lounge of a corporate office block where he wasn't a member. And who wanted that shit now anyway? Middle management in the large construction business left him drowning in a bureaucracy where his colleagues above ignored him, and those below fought to get past him. Or worse still, ignored him too. And home, that used to be where he'd find refuge, but now it was just the same, fights, fuck-ups and failure. Hayley – oh Christ, his one perfect project, his beautiful girl! – off the rails.

Once upon a time Haley and Mick had been good together. The fairy story held true for those first few years, and they used to laugh a lot, Michelle too. He'd loved being a dad, his beautiful baby casually cradled in his arm as he sat outside the pub and yarned with friends. He was there for her first steps, anxiously resisting the urge to help her up every time she fell, landing with a plop on fat nappy-padded buttocks. The sleepless nights, with her teething screams and childish nightmares, he wore like a badge of honour, the pride of being a father shared through bleary eyes at smoko the next day. The challenges of parenting a young child were at least a social challenge, and those empathetic looks from other parents at Haley's two-year-old tantrums in the supermarket were enough to carry them over those years and into the golden ages of four to eight. Mick took delight in the childhood wonder and inquisitiveness that Haley displayed at the sight of worms in the garden, crazy-shaped rocks by the sea, wooden offcuts in the workshop, even leeches wriggling on her arm after a walk in the bush. They developed a kind of telepathy between them and at the dinner table would sometimes burst out laughing simultaneously seemingly without cause, to Michelle's puzzlement and, increasingly, her sense of exclusion.

Even when Haley was a little older and off playing in the park down the street with friends, Mick only had to whistle their coded bird call and she would prick up her ears and reply, a lilting mimicry of a currawong, safe in the knowledge that her dad was watching over her even when she was out of sight. Only once had she truly got lost, wandering off at the agricultural show when she was nine to gaze with longing at the other kids on the roller coaster. When she turned back to her father she was met with a wall of strangers and fear had gripped her heart. It had gripped Mick's too, and for half an hour he searched frantically, meeting with Michelle at their appointed rendezvous empty-handed and guilt-ridden. His wife's panicked response and lashing contempt had shocked him, and though Haley was found safe a few minutes later, the speed with which Michelle turned on him had scarred him. He was scared too, at seeing how tenuous his grip on Haley really was.

As Haley headed towards her teens she still used to cuddle up to Mick and tell him things she didn't share with her mother, little tales of adventure and daring, little transgressions from the rules laid down by Michelle that he'd let slide, much to Haley's delight and Michelle's irritation. But Michelle was also busy with Frankie by then and Mick felt she used the baby as a cop-out from the challenges Haley presented. Frankie became Michelle's 'little man' and she gave up competing with her daughter for Mick's affection. It was around that time that Haley learnt the subtle art of playing one parent off against the other. Innocently, in her youthful egocentricity, she inadvertently pushed her parents further apart, accentuating their own burgeoning mistrust of each other.

When Haley reached her teens her desire for independence and larger adventures became a struggle for Mick. His growing need for significance in his own life, which focused too greatly on her, started to burden Haley and she responded to his entreaties with either sullenness or defiance. Belatedly, he struggled to offer the structure she had voicelessly craved, but often came down too heavy handed. He tried playing their old games, but she found them, and him, embarrassing. Sometimes, watching his fiery daughter from across the room, gazing at her like an astronomer across vast distances, he would wonder whether he had unwittingly caused it all by naming her after a comet.

—

Mick knocked on Haley's door and without waiting, pushed it open. Gazing around the teenage mess, the *Girlfriend* and *Cleo* magazines scattered on the floor, posters of pop stars crowding the walls, he saw she wasn't there. Now he was really pissed off.

'She's gone. She's not here. You let her go.'

He wheeled angrily around to Michelle, who stood at the end of the corridor with a worried look.

'She must have gone out the window. I didn't hear her. I thought she was in her room.'

'Well she isn't. How was she getting to the party? Where is it?'

'Jordan's brother was going to give them a lift. I don't know where it is.'

'You don't even know where the fucking party is?' Mick threw a disgusted look at her. 'She goes out, dressed like a tart, and you don't even bother to find out where she's going!'

'Well, did you?'

They looked at each other, wanting to blame but recognising their own guilt. They had been feeling it for so long now. Out of touch with their daughter, with parenting, with all of it.

—

Haley slid nervously back into the rear seat of the car, cradling a Bacardi and Coke in one hand and her jacket in the other. Her bare shoulders gleamed briefly before the interior light went out as Jordan's brother Luke slid in beside her and closed the door. She felt his eyes on her skin and she shivered, heart beating way too loud, heat rising up her chest.

'I thought we were going for a ride?' she said, arching her back just a little, her tank top tightening.

'You can ride me any day, girl,' Luke replied, his beery breath stale but not unwelcome.

Haley punched him lightly on the chest, felt the solidness of him, the manliness. Her breathing quickened.

'Dickhead. You know what I meant.'

'And so do you.'

He slid his hand up her thigh to the edge of the miniskirt but she pushed it back, wanting to savour this feeling of being desired, make it last. It was all new territory. She wanted a kiss.

'Come on Hales, you're not Daddy's girl now.' Luke's hand returned, more insistent.

Haley felt the dig and her mood slipped a little. What right did Luke have to say that? Her dad could knock him out in one hit if he wanted to. And she was her own girl anyway. But she wondered what her dad would say, now, about this. That she was wasting herself on the likes of Luke Heany. He expected a lot of her, her dad, and she felt the pride and the prison of this in equal measure. She pushed Luke's hand away again and reached for the door.

—

By the time the eleven thirty curfew passed they stopped leaving messages on Haley's mobile and Jordan's parents' answering machine. They both sat in the living room, Michelle on the sofa, Mick on his leather recliner, saying little, the house oppressive in the heat. Mick tried to censor the images in his head: Haley being felt up by some slimeball twenty-year-old with spotty skin and designer stubble, Haley lying bleeding by the road, Haley with ripped miniskirt, crying. Haley dead. But no matter how much he tried, the images kept rolling, a film clip of teenage parental horror.

At twelve thirty they called the police to ask if there'd been any accidents in the area involving Jordan's brother's car, a blue Commodore with a flame-painted bonnet, and waited anxiously as the duty constable checked records. No reports had come through. Yet.

Michelle sat huddled in the corner of the sofa, nervously fiddling with the cordless phone, her face strained, her eyes flittering back and forth between Mick and the door.

'You blame me, don't you?' she asked, punishing herself already.

'We don't know what's happened,' he said, his voice flat, disengaged, though the fear was easy to hear. Haley, for all her waywardness, had never been this late past a curfew. She wasn't really a bad kid.

'I should have gone to her,' Michelle continued. 'I should have made her see the dangers.'

'Too late for that.'

Mick wasn't ready to let his wife off the hook, because he didn't want the alternative to take hold. That it was his fault for yelling at Haley, his fault for criticising her looks, his fault for being a crap father.

—

By one fifteen the TV was silent. They sat in the half dark of the lava lamp, numb with worry. Outside the streetlights cast a shadowed glow over the yard, shining dully off neighbours' parked cars and revealing the empty black ribbon of the road. Nothing moved. The sound of a car turning down their street brought both their bodies up tense and they held a collective breath, but it moved on past their house with a fading rumble. The silence closed in around them again and they slumped back into the cushions with a shush of air, unsure if the car's passing had been a relief or not. Other night sounds filled the space: cicadas, the creak of the house cooling, the low, humming *ooom-ooom-ooom* of a tawny frogmouth. Mick got up and made them both a cup of tea, sitting back down next to Michelle and gently taking her hand.

Finally a car pulled up in the drive and they heard a door clicking carefully closed. Mick glanced at the wall clock. One thirty-one. For a moment he was transfixed, his mind short-circuiting on this deadly important triviality. Michelle looked at him expectantly but neither of them moved towards the door. Footsteps on the porch: irregular, soft. The fly screen door squeaked minutely on its hinge and then a pause.

—

Haley closed the screen door gently and crept further down the porch to Frankie's window. She couldn't find her key and didn't want to knock. Her lipstick was smeared and the Cool Mints questionable. She didn't want to end such a good night being roused on by her parents. She knew it was coming, but she just hoped she could delay the shit hitting the fan until she felt more sober in the morning. Pushing aside the screen locks through the torn mesh, she slid the screen open and swung her legs over the sill, grimacing a little at the pain. Avoiding

Frankie's scattered toys, she tiptoed over to the door and was almost there when it opened and her father's outline loomed, haloed in the hall light, her mother behind him.

'Where the hell have you been?'

'Sshh Mick, you'll wake Frankie, let her through.'

Michelle put a hand on his shoulder to encourage him back.

Haley turned to look at her brother's bed. The pale streetlight shone on smooth empty sheets.

'Where's Frankie?' she asked.

The Young Man as a Poet

1980

JOHN WASN'T A VERY GOOD name for a poet. Not these days. Now one needed something with a little more flavour, a little pizazz, greater street cred, but after spending countless afternoons worrying about his name, he'd finally given up. 'John', he wrote at the end of the verse. Done. Donne. A wry, rare smile turned his thin lips, and he placed the heavily annotated sheaf of paper into his journal with the others to type out later.

—

John Ferguson was twenty-two and wanted to be taken seriously. He'd studied, travelled, experienced things, seen death (tangentially), and believed he'd gained some deep insights. He felt deeply, thought deeply, lived deeply (perhaps).

He saw things that made him uncertain: the beer-stained

remains of the evening on the inner-city pavement as he walked home alone, the streets empty except for those sporadic pools of light and mayhem spilling from pubs. The anarchic laughter, vomit and fondled flesh. The depthless voids of nightclubs and ruby-lit strip joints with edgy doormen spruiking hidden pleasures. Grey, shuffling men checking bins, cocooned or caged in their hunger and homelessness. And further out, the quiet terraced streets with shuttered windows and upturned recycling bins, dog-food cans marooned in the gutters along with washed-down shit. Out in the depths, he floated, tensely.

—

He spent a lot of time writing about his observations, trying to discover, or manifest, some deeper significance. Tiny weeds in the cracks in the pavement, the old man in the tattered suit on the bench as he cut quickly across the park, the early dew forming in morning hours, seagulls washing in the fountain, children crying at fleeing balloons, bird shit on the marble Greco-Roman sculptures. Hours walking around the city: the purposeful ones to and from the bookshop where he worked part-time, the aimless ones just walking. At night, back in the dark solitude of his room, he would write out their significance: the weeds broke apart humanity's attempts to subjugate nature; the old man's suit spoke so poignantly of the failure of capitalism; a fleeing balloon, a lost childhood.

—

He also saw the girl in the café.

He'd stop in after work for a solitary cappuccino, sit by the window ostensibly writing, but watching her serve and chat with other customers. He looked at her often, surreptitiously taking in her pale melancholy face and the curve of her nose, her straight black hair, the way she would wipe her hands on her apron. Thin hands, delicate hands, intelligent hands, nails deep red. He watched the way she moved about the café, flowing gracefully between tables juggling cups and avoiding stares.

She was beautiful, had wonderful breasts. They swung enticingly under her loose shirt but he didn't allow himself too long a look, too often a look. He struggled a little to avert his eyes. Fearful of contempt, wrote a bit more when he was in danger of a returned gaze.

He went to the café frequently but failed to speak to her beyond a simple coffee order, hoping instead she'd ask him something, anything. He carefully scattered poems about on the table as he wrote in his journal, poems he thought showed his sensitivity, his intelligence, better than the rest of him could express. The rest of him was too troubling.

The poem he had just finished was one he would love her to read. It was about Troy, the long siege, the Trojan horse offering: the fall. About travelling home to his share house, past the café. About laying siege to her beauty. He wouldn't tell her that, but hoped she'd understand the poetic references, the carefully placed allusions. He wasn't very optimistic; she hadn't glanced at all the other poems he'd left about. Beyond the coffee ordering, she'd never actually spoken to him.

—

John was working up to a poetry reading at the local pub down the road. He'd been working up to it for almost a year now, going along each month with a feeling of trepidation, trying to imagine how he could do it. If he could do it: get up there and read his work. He'd sit towards the back of the room, huddled over his single pint (he didn't really like beer), nervously smoking (didn't really like smoking either, it made him feel sick and gave him a head-spin), amazed that the other readers could so casually deliver their poems. They didn't seem to treat it that seriously, yet there they were, on stage. Poets! And his poems were better – more meaningful, significant, sensuous, rooted more firmly in historical context. Showed a man's longing for love in a cleaner, more noble light. He worried a bit about that too, the not-so-noble longing. Visions of her rose up – her heavy swinging breasts, his hands tangled in her black flowing hair, her naked flesh sweaty with desire for him. Her body laid out, gleaming, in his mind. Historical context didn't feature much then.

—

A year ago, John had completed a degree in ancient history, specialising in the Greeks. At the end of his studies – three long, paradoxically introspective years immersed in books and dislocated objects – he'd travelled. Like many at his age, he'd launched off to find himself, though like most he didn't like to put it that way. He went off to finally see the sights he'd studied. But Europe had been a disappointment. He remembered, well into the innumerable castle and gallery visits, the feeling of ennui at yet another interpreter's offering of shallow anecdotes peppered with the word 'unique' and then being herded through the gift shop exit. He had become jaded by the cost of everything, by the crowds, the queues, the youth hostel dormitories. In Paris he'd woken in the early hours of the morning to the sounds of yelling; a man in the dorm had caught another stealing from his jacket pocket. The thief slunk out of the room amidst a torrent of unrecognisable words and it was only later that John realised his pockets too had been rifled and his change stolen.

By the time his Eurail pass got him to Greece, his hope that the destination of his pilgrimage would rescue the trip was almost too great. Rubbish littered the beaches, tourists behaved obnoxiously, and the ruins felt compromised by entry fees and their transformation into tourist commodities. Three years of classical studies had shrunk into Acropolis snow domes.

Eventually, momentum took him to the blue-roofed, white-washed cafés of Fira, on the island of Santorini, and he began scribbling poems. In the off-season solitude that gave credence to his loneliness, he spent his days gazing at the fishing boats far below his cliff-top café, the colours vibrant, electrifying, sky sailing above the green algae, fishermen laying evening nets like dancers. He decided then to become a poet and while it might have simply been the wine and sunshine, he felt his newfound calling finally justified the misery of the trip. He gazed out at the sea, across the flooded caldera of an ancient volcano, and felt himself, belatedly, seeing 'his' Greece for the first time. He played with the scavenging dogs, watched shepherds herd goats, visited the ruins of Oia hung-over from a night of retsina-fuelled yarning to bored café owners, turned flying plastic bags into poetic seagulls and came home inspired. Ancient history had been rescued; his present deepened.

—

Jack. He'd toyed with that name for a while, after he got the job in the inner-city Sydney bookshop on his return. Rereading a copy of *My Brother Jack* (first discovered in that same Santorini café) he'd 'borrowed' from the bookshop, he was careful not to open the spine too much so he could return it later. It was a name made noble by literature, yet kept its working-class credibility too. And there was Jack Mundy and the Green bans, and Dorothy Hewett's husband was a Jack, wasn't he, or was that Les? What about Jack Davis, the poet? All fine heritage. Maybe Jack.

John. Jack. Johnny, Johnno, JE Ferguson. Edward. Ed. He'd look like the editor, not the writer, with that on the page, and he'd kept his middle name under wraps for so long it wouldn't come out easily now.

He gathered up his journal and flicked open the pages to one of the poems he'd decided to read. 'The Caging', a vision in a Greek café, materialising now in Darlinghurst. He'd put her in there too.

> *One: corner, cage, bird.*
> *Four corners to the flat archaic earth*
> *and still this room dwells anciently.*
> *Old men, man alone, tired leathery skin on clear glass spirit*
> *drinks, the roof-ward gaze.*
> *All prisoners, bird of man, man of man, the men of war.*
>
> *The air up there, smoke ridden, old,*
> *smudged through lungs that coughed and hawked*

and given out in resentful expulsions
gave little joy and nought to sing about.
One: bird, cage, corner.

Should I say the quest to fly must be held?
The caging bars are rusty but strong,
our knuckles bruised and bloodied that we may fight forever
a war we should not win.
Their foundry flaring hotter, pig iron, we're left with slag.

Beauty enslaved, the vased flowers halved,
quartered, eighthed in life.
At which moment will we stare to justify this caging?
They cannot tether soulful flight my bird, caged and gone.
Dead in my hand, your brother lies cold,
feathers lifted by the wind alone, ruffled gleam darkens.
Left without goodbye as did your beauty, and only
death's caged corner bird remains with man
in solitary confine.

He typed it out on his portable typewriter then immediately dotted the manuscript with correction fluid till it started to crack up under the layering of white paint and black ink alterations. Guano on the rocks of Pompeii. He put it away. He didn't want to look at it too closely anymore; each time, another vision arose, another mangled reference to something personal, oblique, painful. Too many wars. But it was time to try it out at the reading. And he'd invite her to it. Definitely.

—

A month later, John still hadn't braved the invitation, or the reading, but he felt he was closer to committing. He'd typed the poems out afresh, placed them carefully in a new folder entitled 'The Reading' that he stored in the mostly empty filing cabinet in his room. He thought about the reading a lot. It had 'resolved' itself in his head. Definitely closer. He'd even broached the idea of the reading with bookshop colleagues, and they'd not looked too surprised. He hadn't talked to them about the girl.

He started wearing a hat, a dark, short-brimmed, second-hand fedora and, as the weather cooled, a long woollen army coat. He glanced at himself as he passed by the Broadway shopfronts, fleetingly, hesitantly, trying it out, this poet business.

The coat only lasted a few weeks before he returned to his sagging woollen jumpers. The hat got swiped by a drunk in the park.

—

But, on the first of May, with shaking hands and a bravado cigarette dangling from his lips, he wrote his name on the pub list for the following week, carefully noting the names of those preceding him and then walked purposefully to the café. As he entered he was taken aback by the crowd of young students in animated conversations occupying all the tables, and he was forced to sit up at the counter bench. Too close. He nervously glanced her way, she smiled familiarly at him from behind the coffee machine, her dark hair ribboned with a red scarf.

'May Day,' she said by way of explanation – of the scarf, the students, the noise. Of her familiarity?

'Yes, of course,' he replied above the din, though kicking

himself that he'd forgotten. He'd stopped going to the Socialist Workers Party meetings when he went overseas, hadn't felt the need to reconnect on his return, instead serving the cause with his poems and by refusing to stock the business section of the bookstore. In truth the meetings had intimidated him: the intensity of the arguments between the Trotskyists and the other 'ists', the naked power plays and ambition of his comrades. He'd aspired to a more utopian dream of socialism born of his studies, more revelation than revolution, more personal and, now, more poetic.

But he hadn't ceased to support the workers' struggle. He saw his opportunity now, the girl's eyes a little fervent, her aloofness unmasked.

'Did you march?' he asked.

'Sure,' she said, swirling hot milk into the cups for the students. 'And you?'

'Working,' he lied. 'Marched a few times years back.'

He hoped it made him sound like an old hand.

'I was overseas last year,' he said.

There, he'd done it, placed himself at her mercy, a direct entreaty. He willed her to ask him what he'd been doing, to keep the door open, to let him lead her all the way to poetry in the pub next week, and further, perhaps. He held his breath, kept very still, the rising flush on his cheeks burning. Waited. But she simply nodded, gathered up the cups in her capable hands and walked over to the students, joining their laughing banter with equal familiarity. Several of the young men touched her on the arm to delay her leaving their table, and John felt a tightening in his chest. When she returned to the counter he blurted out:

'I'm reading some protest poems in the pub next week...'

He left the invitation hanging, unsure how to proceed. He couldn't measure the effect of his words, sought some instant feedback that would allow him to continue, but her face was composed, unreadable. He heard desperation in his voice, felt again the rising blush on his chest and face. Panic, at such a small thing!

The moment passed.

The girl – that wonderful apparition of beauty and desire – smiled, tucked a loose strand of hair behind her ear and took the next order from the man along the counter.

—

John hated himself. For a week he fretted, avoiding the café, yet at the same time wondered if he had, in fact, asked her out. He resented his uncertainty, oscillated between notions of heightened sensitivity and sheer gutlessness. He punished himself with an image of how he should have acted, how a normal *man* would act in this situation. As the reading drew closer his thoughts reached gridlock. What if? Would she? Would they? I can't.

The night approached, a day away. His journal writing finally ceased. His poems, typed and ready, burned with intensity: his only path now. He went back to the café, but she wasn't there, and he couldn't ask if she was ill or just away.

—

On a Friday night in early May, the Poet stood up in front of a small smattering of rowdy punters and read his poems. For the hour preceding he'd listened to three young and confident men read amusing and witty poems of inner-city love, an older man with a neat-trimmed beard read a poem about fornication, and an intense young woman with torn jeans read a poem about the war of the sexes. It was all so predictable; he felt emboldened. His poems were earnest poems, important, statements of truth. Smoke filled the pub, the schooner glasses piled up and the laughter was light and friendly. He gave up glancing at the door to see if she had arrived. His moment had come. He was introduced as JE Ferguson.

—

The applause was, he felt, condescending and feeble, noticeably less than the others had received. He walked, trying to maintain his nonchalance, back into the smoke-filled shelter of the lounge and ordered another beer. They hadn't understood; it was the wrong audience for his poems. The poems weren't any good; he wasn't a poet really, just a shop assistant. His poems were profound, raw and powerful, but these people didn't *listen*. Why had he thought he was a poet? What on earth made him think people would understand what he wrote? He wasn't actually that sure himself. The mystique faded from the verses and all he was left with were his crumpled damp pages in his sweaty hands. He glanced around again to see if people were looking at him, but they had moved on to the next reader or were talking in low casual voices and drinking and smoking. His humiliation deepened with the neglect.

—

John didn't return to the café for weeks after that, though he often walked past and gazed inside to see if she was there. Which she was, her hair pulled back in a tight ponytail, severe and unapproachable. He sunk into a depression that he knew was indulgent but felt powerless against. Winter fell upon him, the grey of the city, the sunless sky, the cold loneliness of his room. He ceased writing in his journal, noticed little, walked to a rhythm of concrete expansion breaks. Cocooned himself in the numbing motions of eating and going to work.

—

In July, his brother came to visit with his wife Michelle. John had become estranged from his brother over the years and the visit was a surprise, especially since Mick had often voiced disdain for the city and its occupants. But they came in high spirits, taking a welcome break from the difficulties of the family carpentry business and staying in a motel close by.

At dinner together in a city restaurant, Mick drank too much and started teasing John about his life, and as John observed his brother's smugness he felt the paradox of hatred and longing. His brother was still the prick he'd been his whole life, but the certainty of his direction, the way he spoke of their old home on the Tablelands as *his* home, brought John's present life into stark, sad focus. Michelle tried to deflect Mick's teasing, but it was only when they'd left the restaurant and Mick was finally asleep in the motel that she and John managed to talk.

'Are you happy, John?' Michelle asked quietly as they sat opposite each other in the small lounge, drinking wine.

John's eyes misted at the sensitivity in her voice.

'Happy? No, it's overrated.'

'What then, what makes you smile?'

'Sunshine in the park, the beauty of the harbour, a good book sometimes.'

'Do you miss home?' Michelle continued.

'Home, I don't have a home. People have moved on.'

As he said this John's thoughts turned to Bill and the ten years since his death. *Apocalypse Now* flashed across his mind, swamping an earlier image of playing with his brother in the creek, leaping from waterfalls into deep, clear mountain pools. Other times at home in their shared bedroom, eight-year-old John throwing up word challenges for fifteen-year-old Bill to enact. Flying, leaping, swerving, swooping, soaring – Billy's teenage body fluid and graceful in the motions. Dorrigo, Vietnam, Paris, Sydney – the places, their memories, crushing him.

He pushed the thoughts away and looked across at Michelle, her elegant stockinged legs curled up on the sofa, shoes discarded, her lips red with wine. She reminded him of the girl in the café and he shuffled uncomfortably.

'I best be off.'

'Why? Stay a bit longer. Mick was a bore tonight; I didn't get to hear your stories.'

John heard a sensuousness in her voice, watched the way she swirled the wine so casually in the glass, her eyes sparkling. Her femininity unnerved him. Mick didn't deserve her.

'No stories really, just hanging in Sydney for a bit, working at the bookstore. I'd better go.'

He rose and Michelle did too, unravelling her legs and moving towards him all lithe and languid, dreamlike. She reached up and gave him a farewell kiss. As they hugged he felt the warmth of her body press briefly against his, and all the way back home he could smell her scent.

On his desk, the blank pages of his journal offered no comfort against the cold emptiness of his room. The poetry lay silent.

—

One day, a few months after the reading, the girl came into the bookshop. She entered with the tinkling announcement of the small brass doorbell and a flurry of cold air, the only customer. His skin tingled. He placed his hands carefully on the counter for support and watched her, unsure if he wanted her to notice him or not. She did, and smiled, once again that open familiarity that promised so much – and nothing.

'Hello there. Didn't know you worked here,' she said.

Her friendliness calmed him, pushed aside the memory of the last time he spoke to her.

'Sure,' he replied, but his angst returned. God, think of something worthwhile to say, don't go back down that track. He felt himself staring, reddening.

'Looking for something?' he asked.

'Poetry – Confucian, Taoist, Buddhist, I'm not sure. It's a present. My friend likes Lao Tzu.'

She wriggled a piece of paper out from the pocket of her tight jeans.

'Lao Tzu, Bashō, Li Po, that sort of stuff.'

Her smile remained and she looked at him expectantly.

'Hey, don't you write poetry too?'

'Not really. Sometimes. A little.'

He dropped his gaze to the paper she held, then moved on quickly, though not before noticing the rise and fall of her chest, the shape of her under the coat. Fuck, he thought.

'We've got a section on Eastern poets just over there, second shelf from the top.' He made a move to come around the counter to help her.

'That's okay, thanks. I'll just browse.'

She turned and he gazed at the sway of her as she moved down the aisle. He watched her reach up for a book, the curve of her body, dark hair falling loose, the elegant hand on the spine. Her jacket fell away from her body, and her blouse tightened across her breast. He looked down at the counter, then back at her, not knowing where to look, wanting just to gaze, to admire. He felt his blood rushing, the desire just to fill himself with the sight of her.

'Have you read any of these?' she asked, turning towards him with a handful of slender books fanned out like playing cards. John felt himself shrinking, wishing he had read at least some Eastern poetry, but only a single haiku of Bashō's came to mind. The top book was a small imprint of that poet and as he pointed to it he quoted:

> '*If I say some thing*
> *My lips are touched by the cold*
> *The autumn wind blows*

'It's one of my favourite Bashō poems,' he said, and though he felt the poem's truth chase his words into silence, instead of stopping, he tumbled further. 'Bashō's great, I think your friend – I think she'd like that one.'

The girl had already put aside the other works and was offering the Bashō to him with her open smile and innocent friendliness.

'On a poet's recommendation, how could I choose otherwise?'

She removed her gloves to pay for the book. The new ring glistened.

'I'm sure he will love it.'

As she left the bookshop, the yellowed leaves of the maple trees in the park opposite blew in through the doorway. The door chime didn't sound.

—

In the months that followed John gave up his poetry and instead turned his lonely nights into tangled sessions of diary diatribes against himself – great swathes of sorrowful entries that spun and wove a complicated analysis of the unspoken rejection.

One day whilst he was unpacking new books in the shop in that same fateful section on Eastern poets, a replacement copy of the Bashō volume fell to the floor. The temptation to kick it under the bookshelf reared up in him. But something about the simple portrait on the cover and the title caused him to pause: piercing eyes, a bamboo staff, and *The Narrow Road to the Deep North – and other travel sketches*. He carefully picked it up. As he flicked through the pages he felt something shift, a possibility opening up. He needed to move, into the wildness, away from the peopled obscurity that he daily travelled in the city with all these competing stories, into something fresh, new, raw. He needed to find his own road north and as he walked home that evening, his eyes sought out the Southern Cross.

At four thirty on the afternoon of a day in late September, John Edward Ferguson stood on the deck of the MS *Empress of Australia* and looked out across the grey ocean towards the horizon. Out there, over there, was the island, the last stop before the ultimate emptiness of Antarctica. He reached out his cold young hands and embraced the stinging wind, needle spray piercing his cheeks. A single tear mingled with the salt lines until it fell, dissolving, into the ocean. Haiku rose up, unbidden, in his mind:

Beyond the grey sky
Sad nor happy dolphins play
Loneliness joins in.

Lone poets lament
Drinking red wine on the deck
See oceans in drops

Her wild fragrant hair
Poets write tearful goodbyes.
Look! Albatross wheel.

The poet watched the bow of the ship carve through the ocean until the light faded, then he turned and swung open the heavy metal door, entering the warmth and gentle conversation of the lounge cabin.

The door shut behind him, the ship's metal plates tolling.

Lost in Fucking Legoland

2003

So much is just a facade these days: the buildings, the faces, the lives. Skin deep, when inside it's all gone to shit. Maybe that's why the facade is so important; why everyone's working it to the max. Because that's the only place where beauty can be seen. The briefest time we give for looking, like a stage prop: three-ply, one season, but don't get the angles wrong.

Sydney's gone to shit that's for sure. All that glamour and all that ugliness wrapped up in streets full of beautifully dressed people, all scowling. Sky-scrapers clad with two-storey heritage two foot deep and ready to peel off at any moment, to be turned into either a bank or a hotel – for 'b'ankers.

It gets worse every time I come here: the noise, the smell, the ugliness. The arrogance of so many people who believe they're at the epicentre of the country and yet dream constantly of getting out. You hear it on the train, in the cabs, in the cafés and pubs.

Amassing the property portfolio so they can live 'the Dream'. To get away to somewhere quiet, with space, without the hassle. All of them, on the hustle to make it, to play this shitty game long enough to get out. Here, where it all 'happens'. Where the big decisions are made, the big money moves (one fucking way only). Where power struts in the glory of its own image, flashed across the TV and railroaded on talk back radio shows.

And then what 'happens'?

People sink, eventually, into the mean-spirited ugliness of a dog-eat-dog world, gnawed away from inside. Or their dreams fade in a mortgage crisis. Or they give up: drink, gamble, watch sport. In the meantime – way past the Dreamtime – they build horror shows everywhere. The new suburbs spread like slime mould, replicating without a skerrick of creativity and only mutating into something even more grotesque. Huge McMansions that, at heart, nobody wants but are all that's on offer, easy to find in the microsecond a crazy market allows one to look, think, feel, fall in love with – a home.

Thank fuck I don't live here.

—

On the ferries it's another story though; that mob feels this city, and the country, is theirs. The leafy morning walk to the jetty. The *Financial Times* fluttering as they sit portside, the sunny side, *their* seat. Looking up occasionally and gazing at the beautiful skyline, the green of their botanical gardens, the marvellous wonder of their opera house, the engineering certainty of their harbour bridge. The world knows their city – the icons timeless, eternal, repeated in ABC dramas and on the big screen – and by some twisted mind-fuck logic, they think this means that the world knows them. They matter. They drive this city, and as they disembark from the ferries to walk into the finance hub of the universe to pull the levers, it all feels rightfully theirs. Hard work, good contacts, rightful order, birth and intellect: success.

But somewhere, niggling inside, they must know they're passengers too.

I fucking hope they know.

—

Two days in this city is enough to get any sane person down, unless they're a tourist in which case, go for it, enjoy the facade. Just don't travel west for more than half an hour. Or south. East you'll just get in the container queue for unloading at Botany Bay, rolling on a sewage outfall swell with, at least, some beaches and sandstone cliffs to gaze at. And maybe two days' dock leave to look forward to. Perhaps a root or two, another facade, but good luck to 'em, poor bastards.

North. I'm staying northside this time, see how the other half live. A bit of a change, trying to be upbeat about it all. Failing, as you can see.

The annual two-day meeting went as expected, depressingly similar. I kept waiting for something to change, to happen, to release us all, but I tell you, it won't be from this year's agenda. Four hours on a new logo!

Actually, I had to walk away this afternoon and wander the city. It all got too much. Seven people sitting around a board-room table in a soulless plasterboard room, lost in Legoland with only one piece to play with. Fuck me: a logo!

—

Steven Best from Insight Systematics (I kid you not) two hours into the presentation, wielding the laser pointer like Obi-Wan Kenobi, showing off his latest PowerPoint training, flashing up slides of major American company logos like pages from the Book of Revelations, finally grinds to a halt.

'In conclusion then, we feel this preferred option gives the most opportunity for encapsulating the growth opportunities the company is after whilst at the same time respecting where you've come from.'

Hurrah, fuck'n, hurrah. Maybe now we can get some coffee. The others are silent. Bored, stunned, thinking. Fuming?

All very coherent, Stevie boy, all fits together in that nice little schematic you started with, and a lovely little tracking tool along the bottom of the screen to show us where we are along this little creative journey. But mate, the emperor's got no clothes; you've given us a doozy. Do you really believe all that shite you've been spouting for two hours? Is this really the sum total of your creative juices? It's bollocks.

Jim Cowan the chairman clears his throat. Go Jimbo, give 'em hell.

'Thank you, Steven, and the rest of your team from Insight Systematics, we can see how hard you've worked to come up with the idea. I'd like to open it up to the board now and get some feedback.'

Steady on the bullshit mate – worked hard? On that? Surely you're not falling for this crap. You've been chairman long enough to see we're being conned here.

Geoff's jumping in, he's been itching for a while, wanting to have his turn. It's always Geoff-the-monkey's turn. I can't remember a meeting at which he didn't have to offer up some pearl of wisdom – sorry, rephrased commentary. Champing at the bit, nibbling at the peanuts. His firm's into shopping malls now – more like fucking prisons or zoos with tiny cages as shops. I've seen 'em up and down the coast, shiny concrete monstrosities, all proudly stamped with Moniker Constructions. The guy's a moron.

'I like it. I like the way you've approached it so elegantly, so cleanly. I can see it working really well on our products. You've got my vote.'

That's lovely Geoff dear, so pleased you've given it your vote. Before we've even started discussing it. Slam the gate shut before the horse is even *in* the fuck'n paddock. Whose arse are you licking? Nice suit by the way, shiny shoes. Wanker.

Geoff's eyes flick straight to Jimbo after his little homily. What's the game, Geoffrey Moniker, looking for the chairmanship are we?

'Thank you Geoff, other comments?'

Jim is looking straight at Maureen, who rarely says a word at these gigs. She smiles, nervously.

'Yes, I like it too. I feel our members would appreciate the simplicity of it, and it would certainly speak to our traditional audience.'

What, we're all stupid tradies who need it spelt out? Come on, Maureen. Sure your Fred was a few sheep short in the top paddock, but not all of us are thick as two bricks.

What about spiky over there, young Shaun? He's a sharp

cookie and the only other real tradie among this bunch of suits. Except he's the new kid on the committee and probably won't want to rock the boat. He clears his throat.

'I'd like Steven to expand a bit more on this idea of "activating" the brand.'

Go, Shaun mate. Bring up the mirror.

'I'd be delighted to, Mr Wallis. Essentially we are saying that any branding campaign will need to activate the logo with a range of innovative and dynamic versions to ensure the market is exposed to the deeper aspects of the business idea. We're saying that the Building and Construction Industry Training Board would ideally take the logo and explore its graphic potential through a range of sub-stories so that the narrative of your business is fully manifested. For instance, inside the boundary here, we'd recommend a range of print collateral, coloured with these tones, shown here, and that the choice of the tones would change throughout the campaign, thereby *activating* this design.' Steven clicks off the pointer like Moses putting down the last tablet. Here endeth the sermon.

This is bullshit. How can anybody take this sort of crap seriously? I've sat here for two hours, watched this slimy prick from Melbourne with his laser pointer and PowerPoint presentation all very smooth and about as convincing as George W. Bush's fucking victory speech on the USS *Abraham Lincoln* and nobody's said the glaring obvious. It looks shit. A five-year-old would've come up with something better than that. It's a brick, whoopee, a brick for a building company. Deep, mate, deep. Plunged down the well of inspiration for that one, swam around for a couple of months (and $200K), and given us ... a brick.

Oh, sorry, a brick with golden proportions – thanks for that little Pythagorean gem – with sensitive lines and five letters in it, BCITB, whose font has been tested on lab rats. A brick that supposedly represents the four cornerstones of our industry. Would that be timber, metal, glass and concrete? Or chippies, sparkies, brickies – and fuckwits. Contains the essence of our tradition and showcases our stability. It's a fucking brick that a five-year-old could've drawn better. Fuck me, Frankie had drawn more beautiful bricks every day of his life.

Every day of your short, short life Frankie. Little Frankie.

—

That's when I lost it, felt the tears welling in my eyes, the fight go out of me. Not good, going down that path, that river, that pool. Not good, but I can't help it.

You were so little, so light. So cold. When I scooped you out of the pool, so floppy and cold. Such a hot night, and such a cold little boy, my son. Your wrinkled skin so pale, old-man-like, beautiful blond hair pasted to your skull. Flat.

Ah shit, Frankie, I miss you, little mate. It's all gone pear-shaped now. They've all gone. Losing you blew us apart. Your mum's left, and Haley...? Haley: that's another track that I shouldn't wander down. Where's your sister? One letter in six years, countless searching. Nothing.

Fuck it Frankie, it ain't getting any easier. It'll take time, the counsellor said, grieving takes time, has stages, needs to be worked through. But when is it going to be all over, little mate? When does it start to make sense again? A dead boy, a runaway girl, a walk-out wife. Bloody trifecta that one. Onya Mick, winner!

And I'm still winning, all these years later. What the fuck

am I doing here, in this noisy, stinking shithole of a city eating poncy food and listening to … listening to what? What is all this? Look at them all. Jimbo hanging for retirement and a game of golf, his belly bulging, his hands soft. Maureen power dressing at fifty-five, just trying to keep her dead husband's business afloat on school-tuck-shop training. Young Shaun wanting to prove himself, already learning the diplomacy of self-interest, clever fuck that he is. Monkey Geoff trying to better his old man in growing the family business even bigger, and for what, to show he's greedier? That wanker Steven, probably just like the rest of us, doing what he knows best, hoping not to get caught short. We're all just scrambling. Even Simon, suave smart Simon, megabucks and still just hanging in there, keeping up the facade. But I've seen his hands shake.

—

'Mick, you've been a bit quiet this morning. What's your opinion before we wrap this up and get onto other business after lunch?'

Does it really matter? What do you reckon Frankie mate; should I tell them?

'It's a brick, guys. A brick. We want to send out the message that this is a career for young people today: exciting, interesting, worthwhile, creative. And we show them a brick. What can I say?'

Silence. Not that old bush silence from up home, but the stunned mullet one. Paper shuffling time. Time to look for the biro, a rubber, a fucking condom for all I know. Avoid me at all cost. Steven's head rocks back a little, shocked. He really does believe this stuff!

I don't have the heart for this anymore. If this is what it all hinges on, then bring on the bricks, boys, bring on the bricks.

⌐

I cut loose after that, took the afternoon off. Maybe brother John is right, sad fuck that he is, sitting on his pedestal in Tassie; maybe he's onto something. Maybe Billy was right too – maybe we should just dance it away. You would've liked Uncle Billy, Frankie. I used to think he was a wuss, but I just didn't get it back then. Pushed him too far. I never mentioned him to you, did I? Ashamed, I guess, at what I'd done. Being a poof in the army can't have been easy.

Dad didn't seem that happy at the end either, after a whole life chipping away. Except when he was listening to the silence, which cost him nothing. Maybe I just need to let it all go, breathe that silence, dance, leave this building caper to others.

Maybe, maybe, maybe. Maybe I'm just a useless fuck like that wanker from Melbourne.

I took the 380 out past Bondi to Watsons Bay, walked the track up to The Gap, to stare now over the suicide drop into the endless blue of the Pacific Ocean. It's quiet this afternoon – the ocean, the land. A single tourist couple snapping shots of each other, laughing, posing. An elderly woman out walking her dog, hauling him away as he sniffs the fence posts. Quiet, today. How many people have leapt these rocks into the swirling foam below? How many have climbed the safety fence only to hang crucified from the cyclone wire, clawed fingers unable to let go. Unable to keep going, unable to return. Perhaps the 'lucky ones' coaxed back by some good Samaritan? Has Haley hung like this? Has she let go? Did someone coax her back?

—

They always thought I was a dumb cunt, but I can see what's what. I can see the games people play, their insecurities, their failings. God knows mine have been shown to me often enough over the years, these last ones especially. I tried to be a good man, do the right thing, provide for the family – all of them. It's what you do, what my father did, what we *should* do. Provide. I've worked every day since I was sixteen, bar a few here and there. But non-stop. No bludging off the dole, off family, off mates. Put in the yards, heaps of them. And for what?

—

I remember the last few weeks before Michelle left, the stony silences in the kitchen. The way she'd look at me, blaming me. Recoil from me when I tried to touch her. I couldn't find the answers. God knows I tried, but they weren't there. I'd built the whole house, every last board I'd hammered into place, planed all the benchtops, done all the kitchen joinery, the whole fucking shebang. Brought home the bacon. But I couldn't explain what happened with the kids.

—

Sydney's fucked. I went for a walk last night, across Hyde Park and down to the gardens and the water. Tried to find a bit of peace and quiet, needed to do something physical after sitting on my arse all day but I tell ya, this city's gone to the dogs. Some dickhead was off his tree yelling in the fountain, kicking up spray at the couples walking past, pissing everyone off, trying to big-note himself. Got propositioned twice as I crossed the Domain, then got offered an eccy by another fruit loop. Can't a guy just go for a walk these days, a simple fucking walk? Even the poor bloody possums were getting hassled by some kids – who got a bit antsy when I told them to piss off. Bit wary of that lot though, kids strung out on god knows what, likely to pull a knife without rhyme or reason. So yeah, peace and quiet in the city!

Did manage to find a little spot though, by the water's edge, a couple of Asians fishing, searching rock pools, getting dinner, whatever, minding their own business. They left me in peace. Same spot Michelle and I had sat after that first week of looking for Haley; same lights out there on the water, the fort low in the gloom, green flashes, red flashes, the dark sweep of the harbour out towards the heads. We came down after the one letter she'd sent saying she'd gone to Sydney, saying she was alright, but not to contact her. As if I was going to let my daughter just disappear into this place!

But I have. Four million people, where do you look? We didn't find her, and the other three times I've been back, still looking, showing her photo around the place, my needle in a haystack. There aren't any navigation lights for finding runaway children.

I'm not looking now, not anymore, not after six years. She is twenty-two if she's still alive, doing her own thing. I hope she's doing her own thing. Maybe she's got kids. Maybe she's forgiven herself about you, Frankie. Christ, it wasn't her fault, but she couldn't hear that from me. Maybe she's forgiven me.

Felt like a dick, but I whistled our whistle in the park last night, on the way to the water. Not looking, but still hoping, always hoping. Perhaps it was the sound of the water, or the ferry horns, but I kept remembering little times together. All four of us on that beach holiday at Kim's camp at The Entrance; hamming it up in the kitchen on our roster day. Haley singing into the eggbeater all Miss Sophisticated at thirteen, and you laughing your guts out sitting on the stainless-steel counter, beating pots. There was a steel band in Martin Place at lunchtime today. You would have loved that, little mate. And Shirley Temple would've too. She was a performer, our Haley.

Or that time when she was four and was on the job with me at that new subdivision on the edge of town, old Joey Headley's place. She'd heard me say Joey's place and remembered the Friesians, wanted to pat them, her cowgirl phase! Couldn't be convinced that the cows had all gone till we got there, that look of utter dismay on her face at the new roading, the paddock of skeleton house frames and that building site smell, all churned up and sewagey so different from fresh cow dung. Like we'd sold her out, like I'd sold her out. I'd sat her up on the ridge beam, strapped her on, hoping the height and dangling feet would distract her, cheer her up. But she kept searching for the cows, her little face all serious and so sad, gazing out at the mud and excavators and flattened fence posts with their twisted barbed wire. It was a war zone all right.

~

'Come on Mick. Happy hour all night up the road. Snap out of it.'

It is the annual board members' dinner and Geoff's all matey now with a few pints under his belt, shoving himself up from the sticky remains of sweet and sour sauce and cold noodles. All the lads are matey. Maureen has pleaded family duties and gone home, lucky girl, and Jim's claimed a senior's moment and gone off to sleep in his hotel. Probably also thinking he's safely steered the ship for another year – this ship that never leaves port, so little-Johnny Howard-like in style, at one time so hopeful and now so bloody disappointing. Leadership from the stern, watching the wake while the rest of us yank the wheel. Building industry my arse. We're a rag bunch of union thugs and greedy owners fighting over the bed linen while the waves are breaking on a reef.

But this lot wants to party now. The dinner over, the speeches done. Geoff's tanked, reliving the industry's glory days that he never witnessed; wouldn't know the difference between a rout and root that bloke. Even Smart Simon has his tie loosened and is looking a bit red in the face.

It's too much of a cliché to predict where we're going, and sure enough, as we pile into the cab, Shaun directs the driver to the Cross. Fuck me, I do *not* need this, but as we wind our way through traffic up William Street swerving to avoid the gutter crawlers and listening to the lads' piss-take-banter, I don't have the heart to leave them and go elsewhere. Companionship is always two-faced. Twenty-five years with Michelle taught me that and tomorrow night I'll be back in the house, alone. It's yonks since I saw a naked woman.

'Awesome foursome here we go,' Shaun yells.

The bravado's high, and we stick together as the doorman gives us the once over and Shaun leads the charge down the red-lit steps, the neon curves of an impossible girl flashing dimly in my alcoholic haze. But I'm not that pissed, this is a descent into hell and I'm walking freely, if somewhat unsteadily. Fifty-three and I've never been in a strip club. I'm not confessing that one to these 'mates' whose bullshit's rising every minute. A sudden image comes to mind – of mucking out the cowshed on the Sheps' farm with Billy and Johnny. Frankie, I'm sorry mate.

The place is scattered with middle-aged men in small groups, finance fucks for sure, all suited up to rule the world. A few solitary younger men up near the stage, cradling half-drunk beers and fiddling with overfilled ashtrays. Three girls in uniform mini-shorts and stilettos swing around to us with drink trays, unlikely bosoms thrust up by gold lamé bikini strings, their warm hostess smiles focused like searchlights. We're guided to a table near the stage on which two pole dancers are starting their routine to god-awful music, but already they look bored. Or maybe they're yet to get in the groove. Geoff gives a cheer and settles in, legs splayed. There's a smell, of sweat, cheap perfume and spilt beer, and in the dimly lit area away from the stage, cigarettes flare.

Fuck, what am I doing here?

—

There was a time when, on Friday afternoons in the Armidale pub, I would have loudly proclaimed that only sad fucks would pay for it. Only ugly citified trench-coat wearing sad fucks would need to go and tug away in 'those joints down in Sydney' – as we country boys shouted each other beers and slapped our girlfriends' backsides with affection. Michelle sashayed along to our rhythm. We were righteous, wholesome lads and we rooted in the fields with the best of 'em. Young, strong, free and good looking, we all were. Fair dinkum, the real deal, B & S balls and all. Dad even told some ribald stories of his own back then, when it was just the workshop lads, swaggering, swilling away with the sawdust flying.

Michelle would have left this lot for dead when she was their age.

I've fucked up, Frankie boy. I've really fucked up.

—

'Come on you dumb fuck, give her a fiver,' Geoff says, slightly frothing as the peroxide blond wriggles her thong at our table. He's already rewarded her for losing her top, but something about the surgical lines under her tits makes me sad. Her nipples point heavenly, her grin remains fixed, her eyes are just tired. The girl loses patience with me and spins off to a pole closer to another table of loud business types, Geoff look-alikes multiplied by seven. Shaun groans.

'Fuck, Mick, what's wrong with ya?'

—

I'm hazy now. Simon's gone off somewhere, the drinks are sucking my wallet dry without quenching the thirst, and the room's spinning slightly. A friendly hand caresses my shoulder.

'Another drink dear – or something more?'

Her eyes don't seem dead anymore, and she's lost the thong.

As she kneels to whisper in my ear, she grazes my arm with her breasts, smooth and taut.

'It's all right, honey, let's go somewhere private. Fifty dollars and Sofia will dance your blues away.'

Without argument I'm pulled from the table to the cheers of the lads and am led off to a curtained area at the side of the stage. Her hand in mine feels warm; the flesh soft, tender, homely.

The music's playing and she seats me in a soft, cushioned alcove like a curl from a jack of spades. Dylan's 'Blood on the Tracks' makes a path through the fog; of course it's the line about taking off her dress. She begins to sway, straddling my lap, those luscious pendulous breasts in my face. As I reach up to caress her back she whispers, 'No touching dear' and places my hands gently back down on the red velour. I'm definitely pissed now but her warmth, her womanness takes me further into the intoxicating haze. Her naked curves shine in the heat, I trace them freely in my mind. A thousand caresses on smooth soft flesh; a thousand kisses without memory's tears. She lifts one leg, ballet dancer like, above my head and spins around and I dreamily follow her graceful movements from the hinge of her thighs to toes pointing high. As she flicks her long hair loose down her elegant back I notice another couple enter through the curtains and settle opposite. Sofia wriggles her butt against me, but suddenly, the haze clears.

A knife-parting surgeon's stroke. Straddling the man's lap, the girl opposite has her back to me, but on that spot-lit slender shoulder is *that* tattoo. In the quickest, sharpest clarity that napalms any doubt, I know it's her.

'Haley!' I shout.

And in that red flaming hell of limp drunken desire and absolute abandon, my angel turns with a startled look on her wonderful, beautiful face and stares straight at me. The room spins, heaven and hell coalesce, and we fall, blindingly, as the building collapses into a thousand pieces of Lego.

Pilgrimage to the Edge of the World

1999

THE OLD WEATHERBOARD HOUSE STOOD back from the road in a large yard of tangled shrubs and overgrown grass. The free real estate guides lay scattered and mouldering around the letterbox that was rusted closed, and the remains of other advertising leaflets that had long since lost their shine hung soggily from the letter slot. Paint peeled, the fly screen door was torn, and rot had set in around the base of the verandah posts. But the house didn't have any romantic distinction of isolated decrepitude; up and down the street similar states of decay were evident. It was a suburban street still occupied by the old and the quietly poor. A block away, the renovations had started and the yards were being filled in with concrete driveways for boats and extra rooms for toys, but here, on this street, there was privacy and an agelessness that denied condescension. It was a street of survivors.

Through the venetian blinds, the light entered into a world of purpose and occupation. J sat engrossed in the play of that light, the lines that were cast on walls strewn with sticky notes of tight text and tiny sketches of delicate skill, lines of light that joined, with clarity, the stories that were stuck there. Stories of travel. Stories of dreams. Stories of the light itself.

—

This was a period, a long one, when J wasn't teaching. After more than a dozen years in the classroom, excavating the history of a receding culture to indifferent students, he'd found little space for true searching. The pressures had built, the months and years 'off' (dealing with the death of his father, Jessie's departure – *all that loss*, the globe-wandering) became more frequent till the time came when any sense of choice was removed. He went truly away.

He went travelling, though not always out the door, and the path to the gate grew a little more tangled, the moss between the concrete slabs a little more persistent, the algae on the flagstones a little more slippery. Things piled up inside the house as things do: clothing, dishes, bills, pension notices. None of it travelled with him – it wasn't important.

The journeys were long, and a long way away, and when J came back, they fed the stories on the walls so that after some time the walls themselves started to disappear behind the tiny scrawls and fading colours of the sticky notes. How long these journeys were, would be, J never knew. The transitions became subtler, the preparation incidental, accidental, the travelling after a while almost constant. On the notes he wrote key moments, ideas, dreams, epiphanies. He created scenes of intricacy and Escher-like conundrums, trying to capture in form and words the essential lesson in all his travels. Trying to tie down places where he'd found some essence, where he could recognise something numinous. He was mapping his memories, selectively trying to place them in some reordered structure that would make sense. But the further he got into the memories, the dreams, the epiphanies, the more doubtful he became of where he was. It became harder to know when he was in, when he wasn't, and where 'in' was.

It was, by any account, a strange time. A journey into the magic theatre where there were no characters, no players, but where deities performed instead, and people appeared and disappeared. And through all of it J wandered, interacting little but collecting much. A time of no men, but many memories. No women, but desire. No luggage, but plenty of baggage.

As the walls disappeared, so too did the floor, layered under a transient library of liminality that formed a carpet of culture. Some of the journeys looked simple but were sharp with the intensity of the transcendental moment, captured in the scrawl, black ink on white. These were the ones that took a long time. In others, the mist swirled and the text was slender, sparse, obtuse. They were quick, or quickly forgotten. Others, still, leapt off the books that lay strewn about on the floorboards; books of distant places, close memories, photo-essays from art magazines, and untranslated scripts of unspoken languages – Pali, Sanskrit, scriptures in fonts fantastical. The sunlight through the blinds played on the stories, casting lines, making connections which

J traced between the notes with golden thread and Blu-Tack; sometimes he followed the sun, at other times just the light that blazed from his eyes. The web grew daily in its detail and extent.

—

One of the longer stories begins as loose threads. A row of marooned robed figures, sitting in a room with the flickering pinpoints of butter lamps and a chant descending. A little further away, a solitary hut high up in the mountains where a Ladakhi lama sits on a rocky outcrop in perfect stillness while, above, a chicken-headed vulture circles waiting for the sky burial. A glacier-fed stream falls ever downwards even as the feeding snows retreat up, and in these waters a naked sadhu washes dreadlocks that flow all the way down his lean body with ascetic beauty.

Into this scape a figure emerges, upright though bent and burdened by a heavy rucksack, trudging up a path that winds between dense wild rhododendron and *cannabis indica* bushes and bare scree slopes. The image starts far away, with no sound, and the figure grows and recedes with each curve of the path, each gully crossing, skirting the valley, beneath the snow-clad peaks and the cold shadows. When the sounds come, carried on a wind above the river's tumbling drone, they arrive late upon the ears. The clinking, clashing, sharp notes of a slate rockslide that has already landed in the now raging river and the dull roar of an avalanche whose source, when finally seen, is already just a white cloud rising halfway up a far-off mountain that is scaleless in its immensity.

The figure looms, the light has changed, the afternoon is

quickly cooling. The lines through the blinds are diffracting, dissolving: memory plays. The mystic shrubbery relinquishes to alpine meadows and ice fingers every shadow with an ambit claim. Rock is the emergent master. The figure *is* the thoughts of J, whose footfalls in breathy rhythm sing the notes.

> One, two, one, two, the heart, a drum,
> Lizard rock, geranium.

It's been a way station, a borrowed shelter for a month on a younger journey, and now it is time to leave. Summer takes the shepherds higher each day, into pastures released from the snow, into the solitude of altitude, and towards the pass, finally, chasing spring's succulent green. Before then, soon now, he will move over the pass, over the Shangri-la, and be on his way.

The stone corral is full when he gets there, the bleating dying down as the animals find their order for the night, the thorn bushes pushed into the entrances, walls topped the same. Leopards' eyes are distant; desiring and hungry, but unseen. The shepherds, four of them, squat beside the stone hut with its low slate roof and bare earth floor, cheap rolled-tobacco beedies sending smoke from their cupped hands. Their faces are dark, darker than the falling night and the shadows offered, blackened by the sun and smoky living. They are the black of caste. They stare at J without emotion, in silence track his smile, return his *namaste* with nods and foreheads touched, and continue watching, smoking, in stillness. In the hut, J finds his bedroll accompanied by theirs and dumps his rucksack with an exhausted thud alongside their blackened pots. In the hearth a small fire glows, warming dhal.

Later, there is sharing. Companionship.

> Dhal and rice and the stars are our roof
> their friendly eyes shine in streaking flares,
> we'll keep the other eyes at bay
> by thorny armour.

It is dark, out in the open air, when all has quietened, and cloud covers companionable stars. He lies on – in – the earth, with buried brethren, his fingers dug deep, gripping the ground, smiling. He has a dream, perhaps a vision. He would build a 'solumophone', a little wooden box with hundreds of compartments that he would fill with soil from every land on the planet and when he touched each compartment the earthly music of that land would be heard – all the grounding sounds of nature in harmony. And this sound would fill the audience with joy. It would be a joy beyond country, beyond religion, beyond trivialities and possession and empty bravado. Sounds of the sands of the Sahara, the rich loams from the Amazon, pebbles from the Himalayas, ancient worked soil from the Middle East, frozen earth from Siberia, clean cold earth from the Scottish Highlands, dry crumbling dirt from west of the Great Divide. The shrapnel-speckled dirt of Vietnam. The peaty bogs of Tasmania. The sound of joy, grounding in its very essence.

First it is the raven calling, now the buzz of flies, a distant fall of water. It is the air over an eagle's wing, the sparkle of a silent stream, a fluttering prayer flag sending its communal Om. It is the surf break of memory, a perfume of transcendent love, a carnal delight, a lichen's slow growth on silver granite, the sudden silence after an avalanche. The life-song – everything that goes on, in, around all beings, all spirits. Everything once immutable, in-transient, dissolving in the vibrations of this eternal sound.

He wakes refreshed, but the joy is fleeting. He grasps for the sound.

—

He joins the paper squares, and fills another five years or more. Across the mountains, over the passes, into the rarefied air of high altitudes, he is followed. He's looking for the beginning of the ocean, but he is offered up mere pools. He learns to swim but his stroke is clumsy. He is searching for the source, but instead there is a box of pills whose daily dose is metered out by a circling window of translucent plastic.

His prescription is running out; each day the pills swirl in the toilet bowl, resisting.

—

One day the stories find him standing in the centre of the shopping mall, intent on a drip of water pouring like liquid light grains from the ceiling and pooling on the polished tiles. Ripples expanding, Mandelbrot patterns repeating, the moisture being sucked towards a discarded burger wrapper. The muzak playing outside, distantly, the wash of shoppers parting around him as he remains marooned. The potato-peeler demonstrators move their table further off, taking their latest shining stainless-steel gadget back into the river flow of the crowds. Someone yells out 'Up the mighty Demons!'

He shuffles away, back to the house.

Time is circling, it's hard to pin down, to stop the spin in this little roulette game that appears sometimes in another language, tangentially English, maybe Tibetan or Pali even, but most likely, Russian.

—

In the morning, before the shepherds stir and the milk run rattles up the road, before the ice has thawed on the grass, and the paper boy has been, he leaves the hut-house and continues upwards. There are footprints around the enclosure, large clawed prints circling, and then heading off in the direction he's taking. He grips the staff the shepherds gave him the night before (or was it torn from the fence palings?) and plants it firmly into the snow alongside each stride. His footsteps break the crust with a muted crunch, the moss flattening, obliterating the animals' marks. The grasses are coated in glass, turned into glistening sword shards. The patch of soil sparkles like crystals as he scoops up a handful. The solumophone beckons purposefully.

All day he trudges, across snowdrifts, around kerbside eddies, along grey rivulets as the track thaws, skirting the valley sides, high above the river. Occasionally the track dives into a stream and he fords it in bare legs and with boots tied around his neck, the freezing waters wrenching at his footholds and numbing him as he wades up to his chest. The numbness stays a long time even after he has pitched the tent and sought shelter from the storms of dreams and demons alike. His doctor called it 'disassociation'. Another note scribbled from the pad. Another window on the pillbox sliding round.

At one point the track splinters like a braided river, goat paths everywhere, and he's momentarily uncertain. He follows a low track that looks larger than the rest, more followed, easier, but soon it peters out and he's left standing a hundred metres above the pounding river that spits rocks and foam with equal abandon. Across the river, on the other side of the valley, he spies a caravan of horsemen and pack-ponies – the path?

Up ahead, the snow covers everything and the possibility of a snow bridge crossing to the side of the horsemen appears. He presses on, across a scree slope, trackless, aiming for the snow bridge. Each footfall sends rivulets of little rocks streaming down the slope. And with each step the slope steepens. Sweat starts pouring down his face and his legs tremble. He leans into the mountain, onto the staff.

Suddenly the whole lot gives way, and he's sliding in an avalanche of rock and earth towards the river, frantically trying to dig in the staff, his heels, words, anything, but more earth gives way, larger boulders are dislodged, more of the world is slipping.

And just as suddenly he stops. (Panting, there among the notes.) Stranded on a rocky outcrop, a refuge, with the avalanche streaming by and crashing into the river with a fleeting plume quickly swallowed up by the torrent. He lies shaking, gasping, grasping; his heart pounding, he dares not move. Slowly he sits up, his trousers ripped, his pack twisted on the straps, but everything's intact. There is a wetness on his thigh which he explores with a still trembling hand – his fingers come away bloody.

Later, backtracking, when he's finally found true refuge ...

Sammāsambuddhassa

Awakened one.

He undoes his pants and takes a close look at the wound. It is deep, the blood bright and still flowing, but not serious. He scrubs the gravel out with snow, still too abuzz with adrenaline to feel the pain, and binds the wound with gauze and a bandage.

If only the other gaps were so easy to repair.

He keeps ascending. A huge glacier appears from a side valley, jagged steep-sided ridges banking its ancient flow as it ebbs across the aeons. Needle mountains rise up with peaks as yet unworn by the forces that grind down all the gods' abodes over time, till the gods dwell lowly with humility. In suburbia.

He stands with laboured breathing, frequently resting a while, leaning on the staff of sun-bleached wood, his body just hanging there, exhausted, dumb, staring at nothing on the ground, emptying.

Exhaustion as an ascetic practice.

There's a chink in the blinds, the light so bright. He pauses with the pill, then throws it into the bowl.

Some days there is a semblance of stability. From the supermarket: cans of beans, bread, a large sack of rice, fruit. During the taxi ride home the Pakistani driver doesn't say much, doesn't make comment on his shabby appearance.

A note about the trail is stuck to the wall in a patch of sunlight. Near the top of the valley, the last few exhausted turns before he reaches the pass, he sees a pony's half-decayed body, teeth garish, leathery skin stretched across ribs starkly revealed and he remembers.

*No pain, just the observation, without
judgement, and the peace, even in that
body-ripping moment, that almost
cancelled the fear. Sensations pure,
without the labels, and now,
this choice of memories.*

The pass is festooned with prayer flags and mani stones, the chiselled mantra *Oṃ maṇi padme hūṃ* blazoned in relief with the incantation – Praise to the jewel in the lotus. The wind, icy and ripping at any bare skin, whips the salutation away, unheralded. He hasn't learnt those stories yet, and his pack weighs heavy with a month's supply of food only slightly diminished. Still so much baggage.

—

At one stage the electricity is disconnected: he's been out there too long. But the silence without the electric buzz is profound. He buys candles from the Indian grocery, where the owner's forehead wrinkles in concern, but she too says nothing.

Centrelink demands an appointment to justify his social security benefit, with medical certificates, via a letter that somehow washed up under his door. He gets as far as the red brick facade of the office block, then hears the voices of the people leaving the building; they are filled with anger, sadness, loathing. He turns away, unready, unwilling, for that diet.

—

Descending a new valley, the mani walls, with their slate-carved script of *Oṃ maṇi padme hūṁ*, appear more frequently, more elaborately, and he finally spies the whitewashed mud walls of the monastery high up in a huge, cavernous cleft in the mountain. The gompa, a fifteenth-century vestige, is reached by a narrow zigzag path. He takes this path up the steep sides and stands mute before the faded red door. The monks take him in. Later, he bathes in the healing waters of the sacred well that constantly fills far back in the cavern. His chilled body sings. There is a ring of grime around the edges of the bath.

—

Months pass while he sits there with those maroon figures in communal solitude. One by one he peels the travelogue contained in the notes and sticks them to the walls. The search for the transcendent becomes universal. He sits, he walks, like a memory of an enlightened self, a better self, a sicker self, the questions remain, the judgements call. Is he the child, the madman, the deaf, the dumb, the insane?

In the pause, in the silence with the radio turned down, the television off, the family unborn, the script unwritten, the thoughts unformed from any book, he remains out there, searching for the one, original...

breath.

He sits in the gompa, beneath the butter lamps and tantric deities now rendered meaningful, powerful, with his initiation. Yamantaka, the wrathful Buddha-being, flails him with human skulls and the fiercest of grins, but the mental projection gives him the courage to withstand these hell realms. The practice is fleeting, yet the mandala that he's built is now home to all the gods and demons of this world and he practises there the vicissitudes of life and death and touches… the sands of Time-Less-Ness. And the pains, the ribbons of flame that flare from knees folded in lotus, lives folded, all those pleasures and pains printed into the circuits of the body: they pass.

Impermanence – a dissolving chrysalis of chaos.

These were the days of illumination. When a conversation, so rare it was rarefied like the very air, revealed all dualities. (Was it with his doctor or was it his guru?) When speech says one thing and everything else unveils the opposite: the inflections, the body movements, the sleights of hand. The mind revealed, unwittingly undoing the very meaning spoken, because in everything uttered the opposite was also born. These, the vestiges of a transforming self. 'Have a good day' and the offer of chips and Coke, and a renewal at the chemist/drugstore, and a shady deal under twisted monkey bars in an abandoned park, was all too much society. He retreats to the rock-house. The words tumble, the paper squares fill furiously.

The monks rub silver flutes
that spill mandala sands
and we all chant
the same song.

The vials of earth fill. The music is close.

⌒

The journeying books were piled high on the living room floor. Sacred scriptures of knowing: The Pāli Canon, The *Ramayana*, Lama Govinda's *The Way of the White Cloud*, The *Lonely Planet* – and The Knowledge, a test he set himself, trying to get a licence to live. The study was intense, way way too hard. From folded knees more flames furnaced.

At the heart there is the circle. In the room the books and journals are piled up and he drapes an old white sheet over them so they form a *chorten*, a sacred cairn, around which he walks, taking a break from his notes and finely wrought miniatures. His mind burns. The library notices for overdue books go ignored, un-received.

⌒

This time he travelled for months – in trains, trucks, buses and on foot, and was still humbled by the pilgrims who prostrated their path all the way east from Lhasa. Such madness! He came in from the west, from the old Silk Road that curls up through the Karakoram and the western end of the Himalayas, past the ruins of tumbled trucks and road-slips that carried everything a thousand metres down the mountainside. Past the silenced minarets of the Uyghurs in Kashgar on the dry desert plains, still looking towards the distant sacred Mount Kailash that formed in his mind's eye as the centre of his own special mandala. Weeks hitching on the back of trucks that rattled and shook till they broke down every hundred kilometres or so. On a road mostly an illusion, a rutted stony track that so often disappeared on the dusty open steppe and dipped occasionally to ford grey-blue meltwater rivers that flowed from distant mountains and fed the great rivers of Asia.

Other pilgrims joined him. Sounds intruded, and he absorbed them all. The garbage truck rattled up the street, his 4 a.m. waking gong. He was wandering. On the last leg approaching the mountain's solitary foothill village they pick up a dozen wild-eyed, laughing Tibetans in patched coats. Three Khampa youth from the east, braided hair and red tassels, smile mischievously and flash long knives in bravado, bogans in the roofless mall. Flirting married women, their status aproned on their fine yak wool *tubas*, teach him new songs and share old mantras: *Om muni muni maha muniye soha*, homage to the sage, the great sage, the Buddha. They clap hands in delight at his incantations. Sideways, the shopping mall PA belts out Kylie Minogue as he watches teenage mums in miniskirts breathe dragon smoke onto their babes and mime Madonna's moves for other eyes.

He scribbles another sticky note ...

> So little of what I know is
> of any value here.

... that soon disappeared under the layering of time.

—

The last part was walked alone, away from the mountain and the road-head, across the plains to bathe first in the precious waters of Tso Marpham, the Undefeated Lake. Female to Kailash's male, to bathe in the waters is said to ensure a reincarnation as a god. The water's mirrored surface reflects his desires, and though the face that gazes back is of a wild-haired travel-worn pilgrim, he is still only visiting. He turns the pages slowly; this time the notes are multi-depth, the essences un-summable. In the windows of a gompa on the hill, a red hat and maroon robe briefly glimpsed, and as he submerses himself in the water, it is to the here and now he attends. Through his hands run the sacred sands: turquoise, silver, gold, coral and iron. An immense sky of luminous blue lifts the waters so that he floats, formless, between. Unrealmed.

He collects some of the sands, stuffing the vials into his worn rucksack.

—

There is a glimpse, up through the swirling cloud that hangs around the slopes like a blessing scarf, of the snow-capped mountain. As he walks around it prayer flags flutter, sending wind horses galloping into the sky, and the path is strewn with the sacred imprints of saints and buddhas alike. At each mystic footprint, the pilgrims make offerings of yak butter, barley-meal *tsampa*, coins and mani stones, and he too, prostrates and places coins of indeterminate currency. On the north side of the mountain, he joins the other pilgrims and digs into the earth for a particular white clay. Said to be the flesh of Kailash, its medicinal powers will ease the pain of childbirth, cure headaches, colds, skin diseases, wounds. Leprosy. He fills a small vial, to sing to distant people. His digging leaves the floorboards bare.

> To ease the pain of birth ...
> and the memory of death.

The imagery is sharp, even as it falls off the wall. He walks to the bus mall, pausing along the way to press a dollar coin into the hands of a homeless man holding a cardboard sign. But the man refuses the coin, and two pairs of grimy hands clasp each other in simple gratitude.

~

The mandala manifests with each step, each breath, each thought. At the mountain pass he sheds the last old item of clothing, a beloved woollen jumper knitted by his mother, and places it gently with the other offerings that signify the turning of the cycle of rebirth. A place of shedding.

She had spun at night, up there on the Tablelands, the clinking turn of her wheel the only sound, clickity clack, clickity clack, clickity clack. The smell and the greasy feel of lanolin. He would silently pass the rolled-up carded wool to her as her hands emptied and formed sacred mudras without her knowing. He sees this now, as he smiles at another mother, she who saves, the *dolma* with a distaff and a wrap full of sheep's wool, returning a toothless grin that laughs at her approaching demise ... she intones her own release: '*om tare tuttare ture soha*', 'I prostrate to the Liberator, Mother of all the Victorious Ones' ... he joins in, but his breath is laboured in the thin air.

~

On the other side, the Tablelands dissolve. The pill dispenser is empty now, the shaman's rattle silenced. Elsewhere, the solumophone fills slowly.

—

If this was the centre, then the years had spun him outwards, away to the edges of the earth, still building the mandala. Children are buried there, and lovers lost and found. All four walls are almost completely covered now, and the gold thread stretches between the walls and circles the pile of books, binding them ever tighter. Outside the sound of helicopters (gunships?) hammers low, pressing into his skull. The ceiling paint is flaking, and the mould advances. The sculptured rosette is more beautiful and intricately formed than he'd ever noticed.

—

The wheel is spinning; it is hard to find the stopping points. The serious secrets of a smiling abbot of Tashi Lhunpo Monastery who disappears under the watchful eye of the Public Security Bureau – for finding a boy! In an occupied country where does trust lie? It is hard to roll the journey back; it has been a long time since he was sure where the beginning was.

—

He reworks the imagery, the notes, the story; it consumes all his attention.

—

The nurse said he was getting better so he chose to sit for a while in a cave with an ageless hermit. In the darkness of the deep rock cleft the meditator's tiny dwelling was furnished with only a bedroll, a cooking pot and small store of foodstuffs, and a scattering of religious iconography. The meditator's face was weathered beyond age, the skin on his bald head stretched tight, his movements fluid, efficient and serene. It had been a long time since he had needed to see the light outside.

These are not characters on this journey; rather they are brilliant points of life-like stars that live eternal. In a conversation, in the language of sacred texts, J and the meditator share stories of pilgrimage and place across the mountains and the ages. He hadn't told a soul about his journeys. The ambiguities were left – uniting.

'Kaba payga?

'Where am I going? On pilgrimage.'

'Kaba?

'To where? To here ... with you.'

'Ka-re ton-la?'

'Why? To be here, only.'

'La-pa!'

'Lose the baggage!'

J's mind is too full of sights–see–ing. The meditator knows. He offers J a nearby cleft cave to sleep in, a sleep broken by the sounds of rustling in the night, and dreams. He laughs! J smiles, picks up a feather and presses it into the pages of his journal. Collects more sand for the vials.

'We part: kaleh sho I say, kaleh pey he returns: sit well, go well. We do both, simultaneously.'

Eventually the stories spun him outwards: out of the house, back onto the trail, wandering the world to its waterfall edges. He had built the centre of the mandala and now he needed the stories for the surrounds, something to define the edges. But there were times when the precipices were vertiginous. A time in Barrow, Alaska, standing on the last piece of terra firma among the bones of bowhead whales that had been hunted and flensed by the locals and now lay bleaching in the circling summer light. The great curved ribs were cemented into the permafrost and rose out of the slush, framing the expanse of frozen sea heading north. He gazed out towards the Pole. He stood letting the wind whip his face, his fingers and feet numb, staring out into the distance, trying to find the line where the white sea met the white sky, a line that would give some semblance of order to this chaos. But he could find nothing. For hours he stood staring, as the local Yupik men in turn stared out of their windows towards this strange visitor, keeping an eye on him, and the approaching polar bears, as he slowly froze. He was brought back by a kid on a BMX bike, riding along on the ocean and doing jumps off the sastrugi, who skidded to a halt in front of J and asked, with a friendly, quizzical look; '*Waqaa?*' What's up?

In the park, on the concrete, other BMX riders flew off the smooth tops of the half-pipe. On the walls in the house the sunlight threaded more lines between these stars, forming constellations of bears, bogans and bikes. He was making his own symbols, lost in that interplay of the living godhead and the iconography of others. But his mind un-formed and eventually he placed it among the sparser rooms of the mandala that still accompanied him.

Dropping
I pick up my mind
And dust it away

These were the rooms he kept returning to. In that weatherboard house two rooms remained virtually empty: one with only a sitting cushion and the shawl, and the other a pure white room empty but for a window that gathered in the most light of anywhere in the house. When the clutter of the sticky notes and piled books drove him, shaking, for greater refuge, he retreated to these rooms, the white one in particular, and sat absorbing the rays.

—

One day the dizziness drove him into the white room and there, curled in the centre of the room, was a black cat. He looked at it in surprise, this other living creature in a house so accustomed to his sole occupancy. The cat was sleek, shiny, well groomed and alert, but completely relaxed. It stared back at him with watchful eyes but made no move to leave the spot of warmth where it lay, sun bright in the white room. He could hear its purring. He leaned down to stroke its fur and it uncurled itself slowly, stood, stretched and rubbed up against him with an inexplicable familiarity. J could feel its purr vibrating through its body, up his leg, into his chest. He turned, the earth's edges smoothed over just enough, and he walked into the chaos of the kitchen and found some milk.

—

Caring for the cat (who didn't need caring for and who wore the name tag, Schrödinger) kept J out of the sticker room for longer periods each day, since it refused to join him there, and he sought it out in the white room or in the garden. He found himself more and more often sitting quietly on the verandah stroking its fur, letting it leap on and off his lap as he daydreamed, nodding now to the passers-by who smiled through furtive glances, caught in surprise by his acknowledgement. He cleared a path through the tangled garden to a boulder that lay up against an old gum tree, and settled himself and the cat each day on this rock to soak in the sun, planting his bare feet deep in the earth.

—

On the last journey he passed through the centre of the country and camped alongside another rock. The towering presence of Uluru awoke in him something primordial, but still he was a traveller to the sounds of the distant clap sticks calling. Before sunrise the Southern Cross gleamed above the Rock's darkness and he watched the light slowly turn out the stars and ignite the red stone, heralding the day with burning intensity. He poured desert sands through his hands, ignoring the last vial. The sticky note showed an almost childlike picture of the Rock, coloured Texta red.

—

When he finally stepped back on the heart-shaped island of Lutruwita Tasmania so much time had disappeared. As he waited at the airport for his battered rucksack to appear, he searched the swirl of faces for some familiarity across those distant weathered years. But neither the luggage trolley that trundled in from the plane nor the faces delivered anything familiar. He waited long past the time when all the other travellers had collected their luggage and the trolley stood empty, its flat galvanised steel surfaces cold in the early spring air, his rucksack nowhere to be seen. Eventually, he walked out of the terminal into the sun and let the warmth flood his travel-scarred body and mind. He burst out laughing and, smiling broadly, waved at a taxi and climbed in.

'Moonah, thanks mate,' he said, naming the suburb of his home, the Aboriginal word now wrapped in his mind around an old weatherboard house.

'Ya travelling light cobber. Where ya been?' the cabbie asked.

'Round about. Checking out some stories. You know how it is.'

'Too right cobber, too right. Heaps of shit going down, aye? Nah, I tell ya, ya don't wanna go wandering too far these days; we should all be keepin' mum and staying tight. And them others should be too, not trying to flog our jobs by showing up on our shores – bloody illegals the lot of them. And another thing, I'll tell ya who is *really* responsible for them 9/11 bombings ...'

He let the tirade wash past him and sat staring through the windscreen at the looming mountain. When they arrived at the house, Schrödinger was sitting on the white fence post by the letterbox.

How fluidly her tail flicks, back and forward, back and forward; a black line on white, there but not there.

As the cabbie appeared with groceries from the boot, the cat gave a loud meow and stood up, stretching delicately as it balanced on the narrow post.

'She's happy to see you' the cabbie said, dumping the bags of food at the gate.

'And me, mate. I'm happy to see her.'

As the taxi disappeared up the quiet suburban street, the cat jumped from the post and landed in John's arms. She purred contentedly for a while as he stood there, staring up at the mountain and stroking her fur, and then as he turned up the path towards the house, she vanished. John chuckled quietly and opened the door, letting the light stream in. Caught by the breeze of the opening door, a sticky label peeled off the wall and floated to the floor. He picked it up.

> If by searching, the searcher of the search
> be sought and not found, thereupon the goal
> of the search is reached and also the end of
> the search itself.
>
> —Padma Sambhava, *The Tibetan book of Great Liberation*

I held it up to the light to make sure I was reading it correctly, but the text, too, had faded away.

The Beekeeper's Daughter

2004

A note on the kitchen table, *Didn't want to wake you after your long trip. Beautiful day: playing with the bees up the track at the Bus Stop. Help yourself to breakfast – pancakes in the oven. Come up if you want. Love Dad.* In the late morning sun Haley went looking for him, found him all suited up and zoned in, and settled herself in the sunshine to watch.

He worked in silence, occasionally looking over at her to see if she was still there, but remaining focused on the bees. Every now and then he'd bellow the smoker a little in response to the changes in their buzz, the minimal rise in tone that showed him they were a little more anxious than before and needing pacifying. They crawled across his swollen bare hands, over the gauze on his headgear, up his stained pale pants. His fluid movements were confident, unhurried – a side of her father she'd not seen before, but one she had watched, as a child, in her grandfather. That smoky combination of wax, honey, and eucalypt: the old man teasing her with bare hands full of swarming bees or other times dripping honey straight from the cut comb into her wide-open mouth like a daddy bird feeding a fledgling. The sticky mess and laughter of those hot summer days up on the Tablelands.

Her father had aged. In the few months since they'd crossed paths in that strip club in Sydney, she'd seen him only half a dozen times and still it shocked her how grey he'd gone, how slowly he moved, how laboured and effortful it all seemed. Yet here, with the bees, she was witnessing another face of her father, one that equally surprised her. Gone was the anger, the bitterness, the defeated emptiness she'd observed in Sydney. In its place was a serenity, a dedication and purposefulness. She smiled quietly: her zen monk father!

Still, she was apprehensive. Coming here was taking a massive leap into a past she'd tried so hard to forget. Though he hadn't said anything when he picked her up from the bus stop in town, she felt judgemental eyes. When they talked he brushed aside all her attempted explanations, saying simply how happy he was that he'd found her, but still she doubted. Talking with her mother had only fed her nervousness. Michelle called when she heard Mick had found Haley, and Haley, in the groggy hours of a post-work mid-morning sleep, had let spill where she'd met up with her father. Michelle's stunned silence and her tirade of moral outrage had bruised Haley more than she could have foreseen. The power of parental judgement lingered even after seven years of absence and independence.

Her dad had said nothing. His smiles had seemed so genuine; if anything it was his eyes that made her pause. Were they mirrors or were they windows? She shook her head to stop the thoughts. Smelt again the wafts of smoke, bush incense to better memories. It was time to find a way back to more of them.

Mick was working quickly now, a subtle rise in the hum of the bees telling him he'd disturbed them long enough. With the same quick fluid movements he restacked the hive and turned to the last one to be checked, puffing the smoker to get it smouldering and half-disappearing in the resulting acrid cloud. Before he opened the hive he gave Haley a thumbs up and then opened his hands and shrugged his shoulders. She smiled at the familiar movements, filling in the facial gestures she knew would be there behind the gauze mask and billowing smoke. Her old Dad was still there, wondering how she was: *All good, kid, yes?*

She returned the thumbs up but wondered, *All good?*

Around her, older memories swirled. Grandpa Frank pointing out the eagles with his walking stick, tracking their spiralling rise on the thermals and following the fading dots as they glided off down the valley. Making scones with Grandma and proudly serving them to the family out on the creaky wooden deck with Grandpa's old handmade furniture; the tablecloth always laid, the beaded lace covers on the jug of whipped cream and dishes of homemade jam. The table always wonky – 'Grandpa's gonna fix it'; making a kite in the workshop with little Frankie, from offcuts and faded work shirts from the rag bag; Frankie's joyous laughter as it rose up a few feet; their dad's endless 'fine tuning' to get it always higher.

Frankie ... and the tears welled up. Again she physically shook herself as if to free her mind. By the hive Mick caught the movement and decided to call it a day. As he walked towards her he gently brushed the few clinging bees off with his hands and then peeled off his headgear.

'Honey next week, my girl.' He wiped his sweaty brow, leaving an ashy waxy line like some initiation marking on his forehead. 'You still like honey, don't you?'

'Sure. Never tasted yours though,' Haley replied. 'When did you take up beekeeping?'

'Six years ago. I found your grandpa's old gear in the shed when I moved up here. I collected a few feral swarms and, well, Bob's your uncle.'

Mick swept his hand around the half-dozen hives. The neatly stacked boxes looked like dwarf urban tower blocks in the midday sun.

'It's better than building shitty high rises in the city,' he said.

Haley let the words settle before she continued.

'Do you sell it, Dad?'

'Nah, give it away mostly. There's heaps in the shed if you want to take any back with you.' Mick hurried on. 'Just help yourself as long as you're here, for as long as you want. It's your place too, you know.'

Haley looked at him and didn't reply.

⁓

They walked through the old bush tracks that Mick had cleared over the years, rebuilding the stone benching and chainsawing the fallen timber. They gently picked up old threads of her childhood, safely steering away from references to the years just before she'd run away and instead swapping memories of earlier times, especially times up there on Mick's parents' property.

Haley led her father on a remembered childhood discovery trail of favourite trees, trying to track old boughs and twisted trunks that had held her little body in enchantment all those years before. They discovered old glens that both had visited in their childhoods but had never shared: mossy glades overhung with tree ferns and stream-smoothed boulders; lichen- and mushroom-encrusted logs whose massive rotting forms were still sinking into the soft places of memory and earth alike; secret places that had passed through the generations with atavistic certitude but never by spoken word or shown lead, each instead discovered anew by childish eyes alone.

Together they let the bush and the rhythms of the forest, the sounds of the wind in the trees and the call of the yellow-tailed black cockatoos, sweep through seven years of loss.

—

On a warm, clear day, Haley and Mick both donned beekeeping suits and went out to harvest the honey. Already by 8 a.m. the air was filled with the sounds of bees making their zigzag flights to where the nectar was flowing on the tea tree and Cootamundra wattles. Haley accepted her father's offer of gloves, though he also tried hard to convince her of the friendliness of his bees.

'They're bees, Dad, not bloody lovers,' she said, laughing and donning the gloves. 'You got to get out more.'

Mick smiled at the simple pleasure of having his daughter around.

This time when he opened the hives the job was more intense. Each frame to be harvested had to be sharply shaken, gently swept of bees and placed into the waiting empty boxes in the wheelbarrow and covered quickly to prevent the bees from returning. It was Haley's job to take the full frames from Mick and load them into the barrow, cover them, and wheel them down to the shed. As she navigated the full barrow, with its fifty kilograms of wood, wax and waiting honey, down the track, she felt the pull on rarely used muscles. As a dancer she'd prided herself on being fit and strong, but this was another story altogether. And it wasn't just the strain on her arms, back and legs. This was the strain of a life rarely lived – the country air, the bush, the rough irregular surfaces of a dirt track. Of watching out for things that didn't love or hate her, desire or repel her, but rather things that were simply there, all around and within her. All those things that were not about fear and survival, but about harvest; about collecting the efforts of a world far beyond only the human; about a world that embraced all beings, all things.

When the last barrow was wheeled into the shed and the hives closed up, Mick and Haley peeled off their suits and smiled at each other. Fifteen boxes lay ready to be extracted, more than twice what Mick would normally attempt in a day by himself. Haley looked around the shed at the waiting tools: the hot knife, the battered old four-frame spinner, the hive frames in various stages of construction or repair. Up on the walls in neat rows, the same tools she remembered from her childhood with their protective oil sheen over dull grey steel. The wooden bench with its big threaded carpentry vice that looked just as worn and old and sturdy. Above a shelf towards the back of the shed, surrounded by tins of paint and varnish, a faded photograph was nailed to the bare noggins. She peered in the dim light, her eyes slowly adjusting from the brightness of the day outside. It was an image of herself and little Frankie, one she'd never seen before. She remembered the dress she wore, given to her by her grandma on her thirteenth birthday, a long white lacy dress with a flowery bodice. Frankie held her hand, dressed in his dungarees with a little wooden hammer in his hand, a huge smile on his face as he looked up at her.

Mick came up alongside Haley as she gazed at the photograph.

'You always were a looker, Haley girl,' he said gently.

'Frankie looks happy,' she replied.

'Your grandpa took this. Always said Frankie was a chip off the old block.'

Both of them smiled, hearing the old man's deep gravelly voice. Haley had an image of Grandpa tossing Frankie in the air, showing off how strong he was even in his seventies and with a racking cough. Happy days, sunny days.

'We've got to get the honey out, girl, no time for reminiscing,' Mick said.

They returned to the honey boxes and started working. Soon a rhythm established itself as the two of them busily cut off the wax cappings, placing the opened combs in the spinner and hand spinning the frames. The smell of the honey was rich in the air and their hands were soon sticky and stained. When they opened the gate valve on the spinner a heavy, viscous golden arc of honey poured into the waiting bucket. Haley couldn't resist running a finger through the stream and bringing the dripping honey up to her lips.

By mid-afternoon they'd spun off all the honey and Mick had returned the empty combs to the hives. The bees swarmed over the exposed comb and feasted on the honey. In a day or two all the remains of honey drops would be packed away in undamaged comb and the job of repairing the cut comb underway.

As the day cooled Mick and Haley took a couple of longnecks of homebrew up to the Bus Stop and sat on Mick's dad's old seat, watching the bees settle for the evening. The last scout bees returned and only a couple of guard bees still sat outside the hive as the sunset lit up the sky. High, streaking nimbus clouds flared red as the last light on the high mountains opposite faded. Still the cicadas whirled but they droned a greater silence in both Haley and Mick. The two of them sat quietly, sipping beer and listening. The heat rose up into the cooling air and the clicking sound of the contracting tin roof on the house down the hill carried gently up to them. Welcome swallows swooped about, replaced, as the last of the light left the sky, by the more erratic flight of bats.

After a while Haley spoke into the darkness.

'Why'd you take up the bees, Dad? Uncle Jack used to be the one helping Grandpa, not you. You always used to say it wasn't doing anything for the business and Grandpa should give it up.'

Mick's reply was a long time coming. A pair of boobook owls started a call and response that echoed across the valley.

'Sometimes it's only later in life we find the important things,' he said. 'Or see the ones that have always been there. I guess I didn't value a lot of stuff when we were all together.'

Haley heard him take a long drink, and then the sound of the bottle being put on the bench.

'The bees have shown me lots these last few years,' he went on. 'Brought me closer to who your grandpa was, what this place is about. What matters. Kept me a bit saner when work started to give me the shits.'

'Do you see Mum much? Or Uncle Jack?' Haley asked.

'Nope, neither,' Mick replied. 'Your mother's moved on now,

we send Christmas cards but that's about it. She's in Armidale with her new man. Well, "new" – that's been on for a couple of years now. And John? John's down south still, I think. We wrote some letters a few years back when he was travelling, but nothing in the last year or so. I bought his share of this place, but he hasn't visited here since Dad's funeral. Be kind of good to find out how he's going, but there's nothing much in common between us.'

'Except the bees,' Haley said. 'Maybe he's still into bees and you could swap stories. And he is your brother, Dad. Don't you want to stay in touch with your brother?'

Mick caught the tone in Hale's voice – something he couldn't quite get. Was it a belated callout to a family she'd run away from, or a brother she still missed, or a longing for a place that she hadn't yet found? A place to feel connected?

'You know a worker bee only lives for about six weeks at this time of year. Shagged out after all that effort,' he said. 'The queens go for several years; though I knock 'em off after about two.'

Haley looked at him in the dark, trying to fathom his sudden change of tack.

'You knock them off? You kill the queen? Why?'

'Cause she's washed up too. Stops laying so many eggs, stops putting out the pheromones, the colony weakens. If I don't knock her off, the bees will make a new queen anyway and swarm. Half of them will fly off and then where would I be? We wouldn't be sitting on the sixty kilos of honey we got today.'

'You trying to say something here, Dad? About all of us?'

'I'm not saying anything. I'm just telling you about the bees.'

The conversation stopped and they returned to listening in the dark. A few wallabies made thumping noises through the undergrowth and a dark mound shuffled along, sniffing the air. It was almost upon them before its looming mass made Haley startle, and it froze with her sudden movements.

Mick quietly whispered, 'Relax, it's Wilbur the wombat.'

'What the fuck, Dad,' Haley whispered back. 'You're on speaking terms with the wildlife now as well as being shaman to the bees. You definitely need to socialise some more.'

'He was an orphan. Road-killed mother. I picked him up three years ago, nursed him and he's just hung around since. He used to crash about the house as a young 'un and when I released him outside he destroyed the footings under the deck. But he's good fun. Aren't you, Wilbur?' Mick reached down and held out his hand. Wilbur butted into his leg but then avoided the hand, and wandered off up the track, intent on his journey.

'Doesn't like honey though – which is probably good. He'd push the hives over if he did'

'You're nuts, old man. I'm going in. Coming?'

—

After dinner, when the washing up had been done and the two of them sat in the familiar old living room, each with a glass of honey mead in hand, Mick picked up his bee stories.

'Royal jelly. I once had a girlfriend who insisted we both should take a little vial full each day. Said it made for better sex. I thought we already had great sex. But then what would I have known, I was only seventeen.'

'I'm not sure I want to know about your sex life, Dad.'

'I'm talking about bees, girl, not sex. Anyway, you're telling me you're feeling prudish talking about sex? You're a lap dancer for Christ's sake.'

'I don't fuck them, you know,' Haley said sharply.

'I never said you did. Anyway, it's true though,' Mick said. 'About royal jelly. I mean it must be, to turn a normal egg into a queen, just with what she eats. That's the only difference, a downward facing wax cell and royal jelly, and voilà, queenie's hatched.'

He clicked his fingers and smiled broadly, like he was right then and there making a queen bee.

'You can split a hive too, if you make queens. Or better still, just let the bees make their own. They will, you know, if they find they don't have a queen anymore. As long as there are eggs of a certain age, no drama. They just feed an egg shitloads of royal jelly.'

Mick paused in his ramblings and looked across at his daughter. She lay stretched out on the sofa with her slender legs dangling over the edge. A tattooed Celtic braid curled around one ankle where her jeans stopped. In the seven years since he'd seen her she'd changed into a woman with an unknowable past. What little she'd tried to tell him hurt him in every word and he'd shut it out, not wanting to suffer or see her suffer again. Not wanting the sense of failure that washed through him when he thought of his family. It was another reason he liked working the bees. They were contained in a mystery so strong, the power of the group, of the colony, so connected that he could witness them without feeling responsible. Protective, but not responsible. Each bee knew its place and would die for the benefit of the hive, without thought. When he'd started handling the hive six years before, he had several times messed up the timing and found himself with dozens of stings swelling his hands. Beneath each sting lay a writhing, dying bee and yet more always lined up to protect the colony. When he searched for a queen on a frame of brood, there was always a mass of other bees sheltering her, guarding her, protecting her. Mick thought again about where his daughter had been all those years.

Haley was still trying to work out if her father was speaking allegorically. He never used to meander like this, never spoke in riddles, hardly spoke at all, really. But then he hadn't communed with bees either. Perhaps he had always been telling them stories, instead of telling it straight. She'd be buggered if she could work it out. She took her leave of him and retired for the night, leaving Mick sipping the last of the mead with a whimsical, contented smile on his face.

—

That night, Haley's dreams were disturbing and luxuriant at the same time. She was lying naked on the bed of a lover, a beautiful man from Spain she'd fallen for a few years back. He was dripping honey onto her body from a wooden honey spindle, making swirls across her smooth belly, up over her breasts and around her nipples. Then he leaned down and started to lick it off, all the while gazing at her with dark eyes and a mischievous grin, circling lower on her body till he just grazed the top of her pubic hair. She closed her eyes and felt the sensuousness of his touch, the liquid languidness of his tongue. But then she started to feel more tongues, more touches, and she was on a table in the club and dozens of men were feasting on her skin with tongues that rasped and lapped like dogs at runnels of blood. She sat up quickly, shaking and saw her little brother Frankie staring at her from the end of the bed. Slowly the images faded and the dark of the room in her father's – grandfather's – house reasserted itself. The silence was deep, but again, far off she heard the call of the boobook owls. A possum rummaged on the roof iron. She turned on the bedside light and lay there for a while in the sweat of the dying dreams. Eventually she fell asleep.

In the morning, at the end of the bed, she found that Mick had left her two presents like it was a Christmas morning of her childhood. One was a piece of amber, with an insect caught inside. She held it up to the low easterly light and gazed at the tiny, trapped insect from a million years before. The other was a small, beautiful hand-blown glass jar with a spiral-topped stopper, full of golden honey. Haley held them both in her hands and let the tears flow easily down her cheeks.

It's Not Just a River

2005

JOHN SAT ALONE AT THE old, red Laminex table in the kitchen. In the centre of the table was a cardboard box, dust-covered, dull-coloured, taped shut, and labelled in faded felt pen: *1980–1995*. Nearby on the table was a small journal opened to a page with a single poem he'd just finished.

> *Beneath Mountain rise*
> *Memory, an image flares.*
> *Snow falls on the past.*

He stared at the box carefully, knowing what was inside but hesitating at the memories. Photographs, journals, letters – a past placed aside with intention, like a full whisky bottle on the shelf of a reformed alcoholic. Already images had flared, bouncing off the closed box, and he knew the danger, but the test had held so far. He'd been sitting there for an hour, listening to the rain, playing with the poem, breathing. Calm. Sane. He sighed, picked up his pen and wrote *Hobart 2005* under the poem, then shut the journal with determination, fetched a bread knife and slit the box open.

The contents were disordered, shaken by house moves and car boot rides along dirt roads. A yellow Kodak sleeve had spilled open, and he picked up the first photo and stared for a long time at the scene. His eyes rose off the image and he looked out of the kitchen window unseeingly at the distant mountain. His eyes, his mind, his being, went wandering.

—

He woke just before the billy was struck. Before the ring resonated around the clearing and echoed off the trees and valley walls. He lay very still, wrapped in the warm comfort of his sleeping bag, listening to the sounds outside the tent: the soft reverberating thud of pademelons, the murmurs of voices, zippers slowly opening. Wind so quiet it could have been the forest breathing, the leaves stretching, branches unknotting. Movement in the vessels, shifting flows in the veins of the tree trunks with the coming morning: cycles turning. In the dark it was a world of sound, so much more spacious than the one of light, with a reach that travelled miles. Closer in, inside the tent, the sounds of her breathing: deep, smooth, soft. And then the sounds of dreams being shed, others woken into. Then, with the persistent gong of the billy, he felt her journey back.

'Morning beautiful,' he said.

Jessie opened heavy eyelids, smiled and snuggled further into her sleeping bag and into his shoulder. She closed her eyes and settled again, a mumbled 'mmmm' vaguely emanating from her lips.

The gong was insistent; more tents were unzipping. Someone nearby hawked and coughed and spat. John stretched his cocooned body and smiled back at her.

'Come on beautiful, we're on. Time to get up. We've got to be at the briefing by seven.'

Emerging from the tent, John could just make out the dozens of other tents scattered through the forest. Stars still flickered between canopy leaves, but the light was coming, colour, shadows, tones were being born. Each moment revealed new silhouettes, added a new layer of depth. The towering trees that had held rule in the dark by their presence alone, now slowly emerged as the sun rose. Majestic mountain ash forests, *Eucalyptus regnans*, the kings of the valley with butts so big ten people had been needed to link outstretched arms around them the evening before. A night-time prayer, evensong in a cool temperate rainforest.

The camp unfolded with busy intensity. Smoke started to curl up, mix with the smell already impregnated in everyone's clothes, hair, bodies. Billies boiled, tin mugs were clasped with fingerless gloves and bare hands. The steam of breath and coffee and conversation coalesced; expletives were gently delivered.

'Bit fuck'n cold this morning, aye mate?'

'Too bloody right. Ice on the puddles. Brass monkey stuff this one.'

'Bugger ya balls, Jimmy, my nipples have got frost bite.'

'Don't reckon frost had anything to do with that. We all heard you and Dave last night. It's a tent Jen, not a soundproof love shack!'

John smiled along with the others, felt Jessie lean closer to him on the log.

—

And there it was: the image of six of them sitting around the fire with tangled hair and steamy breaths, in woollen shirts and handmade beanies. The focus was sharp on Jen, who was laughing at the camera, but the rest recognisable along with the backdrop of towering trunks and tree ferns. There was a bearded John, a young Jessie with long straight hair. Fred, Nick and – was it Harry? The other names had long been lost.

John turned the photo over, pushed up his glasses and read his handwriting on the back.

> *Barometer down,*
> *The still air holds the action.*
> *Chainsaw, siren, wait.*

Farmhouse Creek 1986

Dave had lost a camera at that one, as they were dragged off by the cops. Jen had lost a tooth, her smile (but not her determination), her face thrust down in the dirt and boots crunching all around her.

John looked again at Jessie's image, felt nostalgia and tenderness rising. Long gone, those times, that girlfriend. Good times, even with the aggro at that action. He could feel her laughter on him, the way she used to always want to touch, be touched, the joyousness of her dancing, always flowing body. My hippie days, he thought smilingly, unselfconsciously. He was unselfconscious then too, but more self-righteous, his fervour blazed him along; it was only in the middle years that he had felt the gazes and he'd retreated from the world. Or wandered into another.

—

There was a knock at the back door, and a voice called out as it opened.

'Uncle Jack. Hey, Jack. You in?'

'Haley! Come on in,' he called, but she was already in, dumping a bulging string bag of groceries on the edge of the table where he was sitting. They greeted each other warmly.

'Thought you might like a nosh-up, and the cleanskins were a bargain.'

She pulled a bottle of red wine out of the bag and walked over to the bench drawers, rummaged out a corkscrew from its familiar place.

'Three o'clock, girl. Bit early for that, aye?' John said, eyes sparkling, pushing a glass already stained with red dregs across the table towards her.

'Far too early.'

Haley poured two full glasses.

'What's with the photos?' she asked, picking up the one John had just been looking at. 'Who's this bunch of hippies?'

He smiled, the memories lightened by Haley's mood. Since his niece had moved to Tassie the year before, they had grown close, and he cherished the ease of their interactions. She had settled into a share house a few streets away, in the working-class suburb back-dropped by the mountain and within easy walking distance of the city. She often called by spontaneously, bringing a youthful vibrancy into his bachelor life, and allowing him to play the fatherly, avuncular role that he loved. His brother Mick had written a desperate letter (which he tossed in the bin as soon as he'd read it) pleading for John to keep a check on her. At twenty-four, she didn't need looking after and he'd be buggered if he was going to play policeman for Mick. She was fun, and he liked her company and her no-bullshit approach – though somewhere in there he sensed a deep sadness.

'I found these as I was cleaning. Thought you might be interested for your assignment,' he said, pushing aside his reminiscing and sliding the box over to her.

Haley had enrolled in political science and sociology at the uni and had told him about her topic, 'Movements of the People'. She knew from their rambling yarns of his involvement in various causes during his younger years. She grabbed a handful of photos and plonked herself down next to him, and started rifling through the images with a casualness he found a little disconcerting. All those years streaming past so easily! She held one out to him.

'Franklin?' she asked, the banners familiar from docos she'd seen.

It was a black and white image, and the memories and sensations were a bit hazier for John this time. But there was a sense of homecoming in the image of the banners, the checked woollen shirts (green and blue?), the river with the dense overhanging vegetation. The sounds were there again too. The endless, tumbling notes of the river, the camp sounds, the singing. Rousing, defiant protest songs, dozens, hundreds of voices joining in, and the swell of emotion that came with that feeling of being together, united, *(we'll never be defeated)* on the river, with one cause. Belonging. Or so it seemed at the time.

Other sounds too: the dozers, barges, police bullhorns, and machinery. The screams that day when people were trying to prevent the dozer unloading off the barge. The tears at seeing the landing being cleared, at seeing thousand-year-old Huon pines and myrtles and sassafras being crushed, torn, wrenched from the riverbank. The spitefulness in the way the huge blades unnecessarily scoured the earth, dislodging river-moulded boulders and leaving yellow clays that glared like pale bloody wounds against the peat and moss. And all the while the cordon of police on boats and onshore, stony-faced but not unaffected, holding them back. Tears streaked down tired, dirt-ingrained cheeks. The sheer bloody-mindedness of people: everywhere.

—

'Uncle Jack. Is it the Franklin River campaign?' Haley's voice broke his reverie.

'Sure,' he said, flipping the photo over.

> *We won this one, ha!*
> *Wilderness prevailed at last*
> *Change is a coming.*

Franklin River 1983

'Bit dodgy, that poem.' Haley said, laughter in her eyes.

'Well, we'd just won the court case, give me a break. But you're right. I was your age!'

John smiled teasingly. He looked again at the poem, at the optimism that was there, seeping through the years, that sense of possibility. He took off his glasses and his mind cast off too, upriver, a few years after he took the photo, to that first time rafting the Franklin with Jessie and a bunch of other friends and old campaigners. It had taken that long after the blockade for them to get the time, with his teaching and her studies. And there was that sense of wanting to honour the wildness of the river. To leave the river alone for a while after all that fuss, all that attention. Let her breathe a little; just be a river, in the wilderness, without humans. But they had felt, and responded to her call... or was it their need?

Platypus floating early one morning in the mirrored waters below the Irenabyss, river mist rising. The sleek surprise of the solitary creature's body bobbing up as he and Jess rinsed cooking pots. The sight froze them, held them so completely in the moment. In reverence. Jess's first glimpse of a platypus in the wild, and even though he'd seen many up Dorrigo way as a kid, it was like a gift for them alone, celebrating their love affair and the beauty of it all; the universality of it all.

His memories flowed on, in the way of the river; in the next moment, the adrenaline surge of shooting the rapids of Thunderush and the Cauldron. The foaming urgency and power of this deeper creature called River with its utter irreverence for their tiny raft, to the shouted commands of the river guide, to the straining muscles as they tried to steer around suddenly looming boulders, dangerous stoppers and swirling depths.

Swallowed up by the energy, lost in the action, dissolving. So little said, nothing said, knowing what to do because nothing else mattered.

—

John let the photo fall back into the pile Haley was flicking through, the river draining from him. She was flicking quickly, and he watched the rallies, protests, actions merging into a stream of activist years. Years of resistance, measured by the changing guard of co-opted words: green, environmental, sustainable, place.

As each photo fell he found himself glancing not at the cause, but the people. He was seeking the memories of each hopeful group, each impassioned collective, each moment of belonging, and especially, surreptitiously, he was searching for images of Jessie. He was trying to bridge the gap of all those years since she had gone.

Haley paused on a colour image of a rally, Palm Sunday 1990, this time in Sydney. On holiday, John and Jessie had met up with activists from Paddlers for Peace and were towing kayaks strapped to golf buggies down William Street, past Hyde Park. In the background, he could make out the Moreton Bay figs and the sandstone facade of the museum. The foreground was ablaze with colour, rainbow hues without apology. A dozen bright plastic kayaks and a few chipped fibreglass versions adorned with strapped-on flags. It was all very makeshift, but effective. It was a large crowd of old and young, marching alike for hope. Beneath the masses, the road had disappeared.

And there was Jessie again, laughing out of the photo, her

face radiant and fringed with her wild hair. Her image was like a glamour shot from a record cover, the soft-focus face from his own hand-shaking laughter. The abundant joy and hope of that time, after the fall of the Berlin Wall and a Cold War that was melting away. But as Haley flicked over the photo, it was another image that rose from the poem.

> *He stood with The Book,*
> *And so much blood and tears shed.*
> *Sparrows pecked the flecks.*

> *Sydney Domain, post peace march, 1990*

'What's with 'The Book'?' Haley asked. 'And the chick in the photo.'

John told her about the peace march and how, on the way back, he'd paused to listen to the soapbox orators on the Domain. He didn't mention Jessie; he left out the way they had walked back home from the march, hand in hand, arms swinging. Left out how he'd urged a reluctant Jess to stop when all she'd wanted was to go home and make love. Instead, he told Haley how he'd entertained the vision of reporting to his students that the traditions of the ancient Greeks were alive and well. How he (and Jessie) had stood back a little from the small gathering, further back even than the hecklers, and tried to follow the threads woven by the neatly dressed young man in a corduroy jacket. He remembered their growing embarrassment as they listened, and it became apparent how unhinged he was. The young man floated out there, among the realms of dogma and certainty and a mind unleashed into the Book of Revelations.

'The dude was a full-on doomsday evangelist, a fruit cake,' John said. He looked guardedly at Haley as he said it, but she was looking at the girl. She held another photo in her hand, again with Jessie in it. She knew he was avoiding talking of the girl.

'Lot of rallies, Jack,' she said. 'Did anything actually change?'

A glib answer rose on his lips, but he stopped himself. Did anything change? Really change? And who could be that judge? As he reminded his students so often, history is written by the winners, read bitterly by the losers, forgotten by everyone else. He railed against it every teaching day, this journey of forgetting that so many seem hell bent upon. And yet, here he was, trying to discern a healthy memory from an unhealthy one. Trying to discern levels of attachment.

'Well, I've lost touch with her,' he finally said, pointing to the picture of Jessie that Haley had paused on. Jessie was standing on the deck of a large yacht, rainbow flags streaming from the stern, not looking at the camera but staring ahead, towards the bow where a crewman was coiling up a heavy line. A small bow wave was carving off, a line of silver curling into the blue.

'Who was she?' Haley asked.

How do you describe a lover? John wondered. A soul mate, a fellow traveller. The woman of your dreams, the lust, the laughter, the joy. And someone who has left you, standing on the dock, with a coffin in the ground.

'She was, is, Jessie,' he said.

'And?' Haley pressed him as she saw him falling off again into the memories, away from her. 'What happened to her; where is she now?'

'She's a girl I used to know, hung out with. Lived with for a few years. We were activists together, trying to save the world.

You know, twenty-four and pressing for change. Did things change? I dunno. Is the world a good place, Haley?'

Haley looked at her uncle. The world wasn't a good place; she'd seen enough of its slime to last a lifetime. Nevertheless, she held out hope, change was possible, and she was proof: *she was hope*. If I can crawl beyond the detritus on the street and a career as a lap dancer, anything's possible, she thought.

'Sure, shit happens,' she said. 'People, buildings, great fucking twin towers get knocked down. And then they get up again, the good bits. But I don't reckon it happens by walking down the road with a haircut like that!'

She smiled and laughed a little, dropped the photo onto the table and reached for her wine. John smiled too, refilled his glass. They sat for a while in silence, drifted off into their thoughts.

'We need some music!' she said, digging into her bag, pulling out her iPod and plugging it into John's old Marantz music system. She looked at the dust covered record player and his plastic milk crate collection of vinyl.

'You're a dinosaur, Jack. This'll spark up your day,' she said, cranking the volume.

'Missy Higgins at WaveAid – best fucking concert *ever!*' she yelled, twirling away, her body swaying to the groove, wine spilling onto the bare old floorboards. She could dance, that girl. Beautiful.

'Come on you old fart. Get up!' she said, laughing. 'Now *that's* the way to create change these days, GetUp! You've got to get online Jack, not hide away here.'

She tried to haul him from the chair but John just smiled and watched her. The simple way she lit up the room, brought life to the book-shelved walls and clean but empty spaces. When the song ended in the ecstatic applause of the concert crowd, he reached back into the shoebox at random.

—

This time the poem found him first. Haley read it over his shoulder, still glowing from her concert memories.

> *Owl calls, the forest*
> *Home to the still-child's mute face*
> *How cold the earth is!*

> *Pete. Into peat. Winter 1991*

He flipped it over. On the front: Jessie, John, and Jen. And the coffin. The last, the only, photo of the four of them together – five counting Dave behind the lens. The sun shining brilliant on the daffodils lying by the tiny, oiled myrtle coffin. The bush, verdant and gleaming in the background, fecund with dollybush, blanket leaf, stringybark, and bracken. The crisp air still shimmering from the image into John's hands. He felt the tingling.

'Jack?'

Haley's voice was quiet, subdued. She turned off the music and waited.

'It's my son, Haley,' John said, a small tremor in his voice that he caught and breathed away. 'You didn't know about him, did you?'

John sat back in the chair, the photo nursed gently in his hands. The lid of the tiny coffin was open and the white of the shroud shone luminous in the light. They were all looking straight at the camera, eyes wet, shining. They held on to each other: John his hand on the edge of the box, Jessie hers on the shroud, cupped around the form of the head. Cradling their son. Jen by John's side, leaning into him, in her other hand a spray of golden-yellow silver wattle.

'Ten days before this, I was making a cot for him. Out of wattle we'd milled. The day before, that coffin,' John said, pointing. He was silent for a while. 'I remember the owls calling the night he was born, outside the cabin,' he said at last. 'And the wind. It came up howling, roaring in the trees up on the mountainside. Like Jess with the contractions. And then ... We buried him the day of this photo, on the land where we lived, in the forest down south. Our land then. I dug a grave, four foot deep, two foot long. The crowbar blistered my skin.' He looked at his hands. 'I remember singing sad chants to him as I dug, picking out the worms that fell from the earth, laying them carefully aside.'

The chant rose up softly from John's lips: '*Oṃ tryàmbakaṃ yajāmahe sugándhiṃ puṣṭi-várdhanam urvārukám iva bándhanān mṛtyór mukṣīya mā ꞌmṛtāt.*'

The words slowly faded, breathed out.

'It's a chant of victory over death,' he said softly. He reached back into the box, rummaged around and pulled out a small, beautifully bound, black-paged notebook. He opened the pages, and there, sheathed in a scarf of lilac silk, was an image of his son.

'I wrote this a week after he died. So I'd never forget.' He went on, reading the gold writing opposite the photograph. 'We never found out why he died during birth. He was born with a stillness so complete, so shocking it was like the spin of the world had been stopped with a spike. Our little, tiny world. His body was perfect, his face Buddha-like, composed. Eyes closed. When he appeared I remember so much love and deep feeling welling up in me. Huge tears of joy and oceans of tears of sadness: same, same. I cradled his dead body in my hands, rocked his still form and felt him there. And not there.' He took a deep breath, and closed the book. 'Our little Pete.'

Haley was crying quietly, her tears falling onto John's arm as she knelt by his side.

'Why didn't anyone in the family mention him?' she asked.

'Your mum was pregnant. It was the same year your brother Frankie was born. I didn't want to freak her out. Nor you. We hadn't told your mob about our pregnancy, it was going to be a surprise. And then, well, the stories shifted, things got buried – and more than just our little Pete.'

'And Jessie?' Haley asked.

John looked at the photo again. 'At first it brought us closer,' he said. 'There was a richness to everything, a vibrancy that comes with deep feeling, with loss and the letting go of it. Of everything really. You know, that awareness of the little things, the preciousness of every moment. We'd been so prepped for the birth, focused on it, and then wham, a huge emptiness that we just sat in. In a good way though. But then Jessie started punishing herself, kept trying to find a reason, started to feel the bush close in on her. There was a time when we were in the Southern Forests, another campaign a few months on, and what before had seemed like a cathedral to her, those towering mountain ash and moss-covered myrtles, began to oppress her. I couldn't console her, she didn't want me to, and, well, things just fell apart.' He turned the photo over, re-read the poem. 'The earth got too cold, I guess.'

Haley picked up the earlier photo of Jessie on the boat. 'Where did she go?' she asked.

'That was the last I saw of her. She was headed for the Pacific, on that Greenpeace boat, studying the nuclear fallout from Moruroa. I heard she ended up on the west coast of America working for them.'

'Do you think she got over losing her, your, child?' Haley asked, her voice wobbling. John looked at her carefully. The tears still flowed down her cheeks, and her knuckles were white as she gripped the photo.

'What is it Haley? Is it Frankie?' he asked gently.

Haley shook her head, and then a sob caught in her throat. She collapsed onto his lap and started weeping uncontrollably. John stroked her head, leaving the questions aside, felt the sadness sweep her body. She shuddered, sobbed without constraint, for several minutes, and then slowly, her body stilled, and she quietened. John continued to caress her back, her hair, held her shoulder gently.

Into the silence came the sounds of kids outside running sticks along the fence palings on their way home from school. A magpie carolling. Cars drove past. John watched his breath, looked at the un-drunk refill of wine on the table. He rested his tired battered hands on the soft fabric of her sweater. When she finally lifted her head, she looked at him with raw eyes and an openness that stopped his breath.

'I've a son too,' she said.

—

Haley's story unfurled with jagged edges, a wind that had

howled itself into abatement, many times. At seventeen, living on the streets of Sydney, she had become pregnant. A one-night stand in the park with all that she could offer, grasping for something in return, but not thinking it would be a child. Over the cold winter months she'd sheltered herself and her growing belly from the ravages of the cold, wrapped in cardboard and stolen blankets. When she got too big to fit in the clothing bins and climb fences into safety, she'd wandered into a women's refuge. The women there had helped her, been kind, but they'd laid the morality on heavy, and finally, when the baby had been born, she'd given it up for adoption. The flatness of her voice as she recounted the parting was belied by her eyes, the scene still vivid seven years on. Seven – the Jesuits of her grandfather's schooling glared at her– someone else had him now: forever.

'He'd be around Frankie's age now,' she said. 'He looked just like him when he was born.' Her eyes bore into John, and she reached for his hand. Gripped him with sudden fervour.

'Will you help me find him, Uncle Jack? Will you?' she pleaded.

John stared at her, his heart raw to her sadness. He looked down at her hand in his.

'Oh, Haley. You can't get him back, girl. Later, when he's eighteen and if he wants to be found, maybe. But now, you have to let him go.'

John and Haley gazed at each other through watery eyes.

'None of it is here, now, Haley,' he said, shaking his head and sweeping his hand around the room: the bare walls, the bookshelves, the red table with its half bottle of wine, the battered sofa. 'We have to let go.'

The tears flowed slowly down their checks as they held hands.

Through the window, the late afternoon sunlight cast across the room and lit up the bag of groceries. Spilled red apples and purple-black aubergines glowed like a Renoir painting. Outside, on the street, the school kids had returned with a soccer ball and were calling out to each other every time a car came by, clearing the road. And somewhere further away, out there, a river flowed through the ancient forests and washed the river stones till they sparkled jewel-like under the water's caress.

Flame

2010

It is always about love. And there is always another woman – the other woman. Except now. Now there is no-one, which leaves him with what … love?

The bush is quiet, the sky vaguely cloudy, undemanding, the cirrus clouds streaking formless and wispy in the pale blue of early summer. Mick sits alone in the old living room overlooking the forested valley, swirling the dregs of his coffee and staring out through the patchwork of small glass panes. The pale trunks of the white gums are chopped up by broken putty lines and peeling paint. Further off, the ghostly stags of blue gums from an old bush fire glow grey among the green of regrowth. He takes another slice of the glazed tart he bought in town the day before and raises it to his lips. He pauses before he eats.

'Happy birthday, mate,' he says to the empty house but addressing the women who are there in his mind on this day. 'Sixty years – the sexy sixties.' He smiles a little at his joke, a fleeting wave by an ageing man to his girlfriends and to longstanding bachelorhood. He puts down the tart and lets the memories of the women he's known rise, watches as they surf on the wavy lines of the old glass panes. Good times, most of them, he thought, with hindsight clear and forgiving.

Michelle, the first time in the back of the family EH, her knickers still wrapped around an ankle and the sound of her teenage voice complaining about his belt buckle hurting. All a bit rushed really, there on the red vinyl, sliding back and forth – no long hair and Kombis and carefree kaftans for him in '69. No rudimentary *Easy Rider* cruise down Route 66 either, just a root in a rodeo paddock car park on the outskirts of Tamworth.

Michelle is followed, then and now, by Simone. How close those two sit today on his birthday. Twenty years past and such different women, yet there they are among the white gums on the other side of the panes – the pain – on his sixtieth birthday. 'His women', who would have torn each other apart in their jealousy and rage and indignation if they'd ever met. You try explaining about love to women, he thought, but both their voices came back: you try telling men (or is it just you Mick?) about trust and fidelity and commitment, you bastard. And no-one, Mick muses, ever talked about the sex, or the lust, or the laughter, or the pure fucking joy of... feeling; just feeling again. Feeling alive after seventeen years of marriage. Mick smiles, this time with a weary, inevitable melancholy. He pushes the tart around the plate and tidies the trail of crumbs as the smile drifts slowly south. Homage to love with a broken tart. He pushes back his chair and hobbles over to the bin with the plate.

⌒

When he first saw Simone across the room at the trade fair function, she was standing alone with a glass of sparkling wine in her hand. A mass of flowing brown hair fell around her pale face, her tall slender body casual in blue jeans and white blouse. Their eyes had met, and with his natural affability among strangers, he'd walked over to her, collecting his own glass along the way. He made a quip about the free drinks, it being his fortieth birthday and glad she could come to his party. She'd smiled with a composed shyness and said something in reply, the words lost on him but the sound of her accent remaining – for a Pom she had a beautiful voice. They'd chatted awhile, Mick alive to the attention she gave him and she to his country directness and earthy, tradie appeal.

After the speeches, they toured the corridors of the Toowoomba town hall and made fun of the colonial paintings of the city's burghers. Mick hammed up his ignorance of art and history and she, in turn, downplayed her knowledge. By the early evening it seemed natural they should wander the town together and take in the air rather than eat alone. They left the reception and headed out into the warm, early evening country air. Mick played the perfect gentleman at the door and watched the sway of her hips as she exited before him. He sensed she felt his gaze and he saw a lightness come into her step.

—

Oh that step, the way she moved; Mick could still see it even after all these years. As the white gums swayed beyond the windows so too did Simone. The sound of the wind droned across the valley, Mick's mind drifted, back into the memories. Even as the racking pains shot down his legs, a pleasurable warmth spread across his chest.

—

When the call for last drinks at the after-dinner pub had faded and the barman announced closing time, Mick and Simone found themselves walking back to her hotel on a wide empty street. Their conversation hadn't faltered, and Mick talked more freely than he had in years. He'd told her of the trials of the business, his dreams for doing something good with his life, and of his daughter, his fiery Haley who he adored but who was already a handful at nine years of age. He'd said little of his marriage, only hinted at loneliness and fading connections.

The evening air had cooled, but Simone refused his jacket and instead leaned into him as he placed his arm gently around her shoulder. She listened more than spoke, yet he learnt of her solitary childhood and youth in Birmingham till her family emigrated to South Australia. She lived alone and alluded to a few hurtful relationships and doomed love affairs. Her job as a rep for a tool company was temporary; she wanted to work with children. Mick saw sadness fleet across her face out of the corner of his eye. At her hotel entrance, the moment hung electric, but they parted after the briefest of touches and a promise of meeting again the next morning.

What made him feel so alive that day, those few days? It wasn't a new tale for men of his age, but perhaps it wasn't a tale at all, more a moment that kept its presence blazing, drowning out the rest of time. It had no trajectory, no past or future, no comparison. He knew the risks but there was a generosity in his heart that he hadn't expressed for a long time, and such a feeling could not be wrong, he reasoned.

On the evening of the second night, at her door, they kissed. It was a kiss of passion and lust and though they didn't tumble into bed together, they might as well have. They walked away from the room and found a park bench, their restraint from the bed all the more impassioning their tongues. As their lust rose, they made ribald jokes and flirted without embarrassment, but their clothing remained in place.

On the final night of the fair they entered her hotel foyer with a heightened sense of their impending separation. They had skipped all the events of the day to lie on the grass outside galleries and municipal fountains, stroking each other and cuddling like teenagers. Time was threatening to break in and the only way they could keep it at bay was to go with their passion. Mick blocked out his family, shut out his wife of so many years and trod a path that only appeared with each step. His desire was huge. When Simone shed her clothes and went down on him as he lay sprawled naked on her bed, he had to tell her to stop or he'd explode. Simone lifted up her head, said with a sensuous look, 'And the problem with that would be?' It was a raunchiness that he'd never experienced before, and he was soon lost. Together they fell into the flames. In the few hours before her flight to Adelaide they hungrily explored each other, but as the sun started rising through the window and they lay only partly satiated on the tangled sheets, a new loneliness crept in.

—

Should he have left it there? Should he have confessed everything to Michelle when he eventually made it home four days later?

In those four days he drove west, into the dry country of outback New South Wales, through Goondiwindi, Moree, down the Darling River to Burke and beyond. Aimless, needing the space and open skies, the bounding roos. And the blackfella lands. Seeking the mystery, he camped out by the ute and let the raw winds flow through him under the same Southern Cross that still blazed above Simone – and Michelle. Stars above the women he loved.

Words played in his head, some that angered him and he refused their critique: affair, middle-age crisis, fling, adultery. Other words scared him in their unfairness to Michelle: abandoned wife, divorce, ex. But the ones that he feared the most were ones his daughter might say, or worse, not say but bottle up inside herself: ones of self-blame, self-doubt, feelings of rejection. Lovelessness. All the feelings of dysfunction and loss. A litany of effect, his cause, rolled through his mind: bulimia, anorexia... sadness.

The carnage of road trains lay flattened on the tarmac; big reds lay bleeding, wedge-tailed eagles rose up as the ute flew past. The immense sky shone brilliant. It was all as it was – huge, timeless, beautiful and terrible. He turned down dirt roads. The dust rose up behind him and the ute shuddered with the corrugations. Alone in the evening, a campfire and a swag, youth chased his thoughts. He'd married young, and his time alone since had been fleeting and work ridden. There were the challenges of trying, and failing, to have a child for so many years – his parents' disappointment. Even when Haley finally arrived, the business took over, and the routine, and the closing in of life; all this he wondered about as the sparks rose up and mingled with the stars. The heat rose and the land quickly cooled in the darkness. The clarity of the stars was deceiving – satellites passed, he wished for shooting stars.

Was it simply the appeal, the novelty, of being renewed, remade in another's eyes? His stories were old, but she had grasped them afresh, and her laughter and wonder at his tales had made his life feel meaningful again. But the tales were skewed, airbrushed. In deference, nay, in love for Michelle, he hadn't mentioned her much and Simone hadn't asked. Let the unanswerable go unspoken and instead allowed the present to be paramount.

And the present was love. How seldom he said the word, used the word, yet here it was, claiming him. He felt expanded, recharged, connected. In a nameless town on the plains, he sat in the shade of the wide verandah of the town pub and watched a little girl in a pink dress skip by with her parents, who smiled freely in his direction. A teenage boy, fiddling with the sleeves of a new formal jacket, nodded at him in a childish manly way. Later, in another town, he lay in a dusty riverbed, exhausted from the sheer magnitude of feeling. He tracked a single red balloon sailing past above the river red gums from some other, distant, fair. He was offering this feeling of love up to the world at large, and felt in return the poignancy of each and every scene. On the radio Midnight Oil sang 'Beds Are Burning' and his vision grew liquid.

There was so much he didn't see or didn't want to consider or entertain; his wife a blazing blind spot as he stared too deeply into the sun. His daughter submerged under the ocean of the newfound love he hadn't known he'd been looking for.

At the end of the four days, when he opened the door to

Michelle's welcoming smile and affectionate cuddle, he felt that other love: longstanding, comfortable, caring. He looked for excuses, reasons to deny, and yes, they were still there: a clinging look that asked, too much, for reassurance, an enquiry that dug, too deep, with concern.

'How was your trip?' Michelle asked as they settled onto the sofa.

'All right, not much interest in the business,' Mick replied in a controlled monotone. He avoided her caress, then felt the greater lie and moved his hand back to hers.

'Was it worth the drive?' she said.

Mick nodded vaguely, wanting to avoid more talk, but Michelle persisted.

'Meet anybody interesting?'

Again, he sat in silence after a small shake of his head. Michelle sat next to him patiently waiting. Mick could see the energy draining from her. Around him the room seemed to empty, become stale and lifeless.

'Why are we together?' he asked. He looked straight at her.

Michelle turned abruptly to face him, wide-eyed. 'What do you mean?'

'Just that, why are we still together? We hardly ever share dreams, visions, plans. We co-exist, we look after Haley, we keep busy, but what are we doing it all for?'

Michelle was staring at him. He could see her trying to connect the conversation to what she'd said before. What he said – or hadn't. She squeezed his hand.

'Because we love each other. Isn't that why?'

Mick knew she was waiting for a reply but he stared off into the distance, away from her. The silence extended. They sat there side by side, listening to the winds from across the western plains rattle the venetians. Hot, dry winds. Michelle looked about the room nervously, avoiding Mick's returning cold gaze. He left it hanging, the question of love. She sat like a roo in the headlights while he swung his rifle, not knowing where to point. In the darkness, other roos could be heard bounding outside. A tear fell onto her lap.

—

He did take aim though. Four months of letters across the western plains from the Tablelands to Adelaide, tracking that night of desire, his body still flushed with arousal. The letters were reciprocated in equal raunchiness. He started tentatively, a short passage here and there, a word of lust and love. Of memory. Kiss you all over. Sinking into you. A memory of stroking your body after lovemaking. When Simone replied, with her own exploration and license; the feel of you, your arms encircling me from behind, cupping my breasts, the feel of your hardness, he felt the invitation and excitement and finally his raw desire spilled forth: I miss fucking you. Fucking you in love … your body laid bare. Her replies spurred him further. The letters fed the memories, built them higher, and his feeling of love increased. But he felt the words fall just short, so he made her a gift. A small wooden box, the corners carefully dovetailed, the lid inlaid with exotic walnut, the lock cleverly secreted behind a knurl. And he filled the box with the flowers he'd collected that day on leaving Toowoomba, when he walked back from seeing her off in the taxi and the tears of farewell had unashamedly streaked his face. Lilacs from the municipal park where they'd lain, the soft pale petals since pressed and dried between the pages of a construction manual, now poured delicately into the oiled timber of the box.

Promises started to appear in the letters. Of love and longing: the desire to be with him, to hold his hand in the morning, to swallow his cock one more time. She invaded his office where the letters arrived, bent herself imaginatively over his desk among the plans and tape measures, with raised skirts and pussy gleaming. She sent him a photo of her naked body wrapped around the oiled box, her pubic hairs hidden by the open lid but her nipples proud and enticing. 'I want to be with you, my manly man,' she wrote.

At home he contrived a trip to Adelaide, a new business venture with a competing company, all hush-hush. Michelle was excited for him, the opportunity for him to expand, to break the pattern that had seen him withdraw from her these last few months. Her innocence angered him. He felt taken for granted at the same time as he leaned away from her. In the workshop, talking with the company apprentices, he felt his age and the sameness of his life, and the open door of a road trip to Adelaide swung wide along with visions of Simone's naked thighs.

—

Mick stops in his reminiscences. The images fade though the tinge of loss remains. It often happened like this, the wandering down memory lane, the rekindling of feeling, the chasing of something gone. He didn't indulge that often now; this day was exceptional. The randomness of these memories had lessened over the years, and especially, the desire.

He shifts uncomfortably in his chair. Desire, ha! that blessing and that curse, that long gone longing. Now, he can think about it easily, that past tense called desire. His emasculated penis hangs limp. He could acknowledge, now, that sometimes the impotence and a diagnosis of death have set him, almost, free. Prostate cancer – too advanced to catch with surgery, chemo or radiation – the path to freedom! His body, his mind, relinquishing the illusions. The abandonment in lust, thrusting between a woman's glorious thighs, the crush of their lips and the sound of her arousal: all this, the wonderful delusion of a lust-filled love.

Of course Michelle knew, back then, kind of, sort of, intuitively, retrospectively. With a woman's wisdom that hid under waves of self-doubt and neediness and only surfaced when finally told, that then explained everything, swamped everything. Renewed everything. That evening, when he asked why they were together, she'd tried to coax out of him what was wrong, why he was so withdrawn, so flat. He remembered the way she kept rearranging the new flowers on the mantelpiece, twisting the stems to present first the red roses, and then the yellow ones. Kept fiddling with her hair, straightening the pleats on her skirt and flicking nervous glances at him. How cruel he'd been. How blind.

And what did he tell her months later, nearly twenty years ago? That he had fallen in love with another woman. That he was going to leave her. That he still loved her, but it wasn't enough, didn't make him feel alive like the other love did. His tears of struggle through all those months of a double life were honourable, because he loved them both, but that he was... sorry. For the pain, the hurt, the lies. But not for the love.

And that was the core of it. Because Michelle couldn't forgive him the love, cast elsewhere. Even when, after days of turmoil, Haley burst back into his life, and Michelle's torn heart opened before him, and his to her and they cried and held each other and they remembered their love. He watched the racking pain of her need for him shake her body and he felt again a tenderness that he could offer her, a spark of worthiness, a role he could play – there, with her. Around him the sights of all they had created rose up so physically, and he stayed, there, with Michelle, with that life. He let the flame of distant love cool, and let the dreams of sex with Simone fall away.

But even when Michelle and he shared the passions of the bed again, and Frankie came into their lives, and all the dancing joy of children flowed through his heart – the summer holidays by the seaside, the cricket games with his son on his fifth birthday – even with all these things, all that love, Michelle never forgave him, and he never forgot Simone.

⁓

Mick walks to the door on his sixtieth birthday with aching bones and pain-racked organs. He pauses and leans against the hard wooden frame and thinks again of that crux. Letting go. Because it took him years after they had all gone, Michelle and Simone, the women he loved, till finally he took that box of letters and photos, the lilac flowers and faded trade fair program and built a fire in his yard in a clearing between the white gums. And onto that fire he piled the memories, the images and the words, and burnt the lot.

⁓

Letting go: he hobbles back to the house from the shed with the jerry can bumping painfully against his leg. As he opens the door this last time, he feels the weight of memories still pressing down on him. Though all those years back he'd destroyed the objects of a love, all around him in this house of his father's his failure still looms: the shackle of expectation dragging so relentlessly at him. A family blown apart, a body ruined. A father watching from the grave and shaking his head. Perhaps, Mick thinks, this will be a final success. Free them all from the past. Let them build from the space only he can make, start afresh, a greenfield site.

He moves across the living room to the dining room table he made with his father fifty years before. Only one chair is empty now; four are piled with newspapers and magazines. One is propped up against the wall, the missing leg in the shed unfixed, the seat now home to a desiccated pot plant. Mick takes a last look around the room, then unscrews the lid and pours out the petrol.

He hopes they'll understand.

—

They found Mick's letter pinned to a tree near the beehives, up from the charred remains of the house. Haley stood next to John and cried and cried till she could cry no more. She stared at the blackened timbers and twisted molten glass of her grandfather's house, swept her seared reddened eyes across the rubble of destruction and gripped her uncle's hand till both their knuckles turned white.

'Oh, how could he be so selfish?' she cried.

She let go of John's hand and thrust hers deep into her jacket pockets, her shoulders hunched and shivering. Her fingers felt something small, hard and round hidden amidst the folds of the fabric. She withdrew her hand and held up the empty glass honey jar with a spiral stopper that her father had given her six years before. The sunlight shone on it with a hint of amber.

'Come,' said John gently, eyeing the glass, 'let's see if we can fill it again.'

The Survivors

2017

The feast was almost ready. The outside table was laid with a crisp white tablecloth and plates were arranged with generous intent. A cayenne-red glazed bowl was full of fresh green salad; lobed leaves of rocket and curly endive rose above glimpses of cherry tomatoes and spears of asparagus. A midnight blue platter of cold meats – salami slices and slabs of corned beef with chunks of cabanossi fanned around the edge, all centred with quivering masses of redcurrant jelly and *chakah* yoghurt sauce. Wafts of steam escaped from the casserole dish full of new season potatoes, the scent of rosemary freshening the air. Further down the table, a bowl of Afghan *mantu* dumplings sent steam spiralling up into the summer air.

Michelle, carrying the final dish of couscous that she'd just tasted, smiled in pleasure at the sight of the sumptuous offering.

'Doesn't it look lovely?' she said.

Joe smiled and nodded silently. He was polishing the glasses on the side table, holding each one in turn to the sunlight.

'I do hope they arrive soon, they're already fifteen minutes late,' Michelle continued. 'Haley promised she'd be on time. I should have known better I guess. Oh well, maybe we can start with our own drink. A toast to us, Joe. To fifteen years of happiness.'

Joe obediently filled two glasses with sparkling wine, the cut crystal gleaming. He handed a glass to Michelle and, in a heavy accent, toasted his wife.

'To us. To my Australian goddess. Now stop fussing and give us a kiss.'

He took a sip, put down his glass and reached out to pull Michelle a little roughly towards him. He squeezed her waist through the floral dress. Michelle kissed him on his bearded lips as she felt his hands cup her flesh.

'You don't mind?' she asked.

'I am fattening you up for new cuts at my shop. "Prime Aussie cow – locally grown, matured on best Afghani haloumi." Those farm boys will wolf it down.'

He squeezed her again, then reached around and dipped his finger into a bowl of hummus. He sucked his finger noisily. Michelle playfully slapped his hands away. She looked again at the plentiful food on the table, the equally and rather excessively fleshed-out figure of her husband and his smiling face. Gratitude welled up in her and her eyes moistened, a sudden flush that made her turn away and busy herself with arranging the knives and forks. She was so looking forward to this Sunday celebration, and as a knock on the door reverberated through her neat suburban home, she felt contentment in what she had gained in her life, and could now share.

Deirdre and Harry arrived first, then Wendy and her new friend Nicky. Haley finally arrived a full half-hour late, Freddy wriggling in one arm and full of random gleeful energy. In her other hand she juggled a bowl of trifle, slightly worse for wear from the twenty-minute drive on the dirt roads.

'Sorry, Mum. Freddy fell asleep just after you called,' she said.

She handed over the trifle without comment. Michelle gave her daughter a quick peck on her cheek, patted Freddy's nappied bottom and looked with a slight frown at the dessert before turning to lead them through the house to the backyard. The noise of voices and laughter and clinking crockery let Haley know the party was already in full swing.

'Glad you started already,' she said to her mother's retreating figure.

Her comments were lost on Michelle, who had burst back into the sunshine bearing the trifle.

'Tuck in, people. Dessert's arrived, slightly battered. And my long-lost daughter up from Tassie. Everybody, this is Haley, and this is my very own grandson Freddy.'

She took Freddy from Haley's arms and flourished him before the group, her arms outstretched as though she was about to place him on the table. Freddy's tiny hands reached out for the colourful shapes below him, but his grandmother swirled him away. His face contorted with the early signs of a cry and Michelle quickly handed him back to her daughter.

'Sit down dear. I'll get you a glass of champers.'

Haley nestled Freddy between her breasts and looked at her mother.

'I'm still feeding, Mum,' she said.

Michelle looked at her daughter with a slight frown. Freddy's distinctive round face gazed across at her, like an image from a medical textbook. She felt another flush, almost a shiver, run through her body. All the tests they'd gone through to confirm Freddy's chromosomal chaos.

'It would be easier if you bottle fed him. He won't know the difference.' As the rest of the guests resumed their conversations, Michelle leaned in towards Haley. 'I bottle fed you from six months,' she said quietly.

'And look where it got me.' Haley said, unbuttoning her blouse.

Michelle gave a tiny, almost imperceptible snort. 'Well, if you have to, not here please.'

Haley and Michelle stared at each other. Michelle took a deep breath and turned to the other visitors, but they were oblivious to the mother-daughter interchange. She turned back to Haley.

'I'll get you a glass of juice.'

She walked off to the kitchen.

Haley carried Freddy out into the garden and sat alone on a bench at the back of the lawn under a lemon tree, ripe with fruit. Freddy suckled at her nipple and she felt her energy being sucked away with him. She looked back at the group of men and women chatting around the table. Her mother's friends, her mother's life. Folks in their sixties satisfied with their lives, the women large and the men larger. Joe stood proudly by the BBQ, flipping great chunks of charred meat onto plates, the fat splattering the shiny white surfaces. His face, his hands, darker than Harry's who stood alongside; his features sharper, eyes more hooded, but both men held their beers comfortably against swollen bellies like they were born from the same Aussie mould. Man and beer and BBQ. Haley smiled a little dejectedly. She couldn't see any of them wanting to hear about her thesis on the changing roles of women in power. She patted Freddy rhythmically on his back.

In the kitchen, Michelle was watching water flow around the sink in a smooth curving whirlpool as it was sucked down the drain. The final vortex disappeared with a fleeting gurgle. Feelings washed over her, some carried from the day before when she'd walked past Dimitri's café on the main street. She'd had to dodge the chairs and tables that had crowded the pavement, swing her plastic shopping bags with awkwardness over the backs of young men and women who had kept laughing and chatting and never once looked her way. Later, at the bank, a young man had cut in front of her, oblivious to her patient queuing, and she'd just let him. She looked out the window to the row of houses across the street and then lifted her eyes to the paddocks beyond and the tiny dots of cows on the hillside. Armidale was still growing – their house, that had once stood at the end of the street and bordered those paddocks, was now surrounded by other houses, swallowed up by other lives.

She filled a glass with freshly squeezed orange juice and went back outside. She joined Haley by the lemon tree and handed her the juice. They sat without a word for a few minutes, the sun hot on their backs. Michelle looked at the expanse of orderly lawn that she'd refused to let Joe turn into a swimming pool. The grass was already browning off; the summer was going to be another scorcher.

'Do you remember going to Luna Park in Sydney when you were seven?' she asked.

Haley shook her head. She was thinking about Freddy, worrying about his future, her future.

'There was a row of dolls, tiny plastic babies with bright pink one-piece suits. They were lined up above those wooden clowns with gaping mouths. You kept staring at them, the clowns, the dolls, wouldn't leave that stall even when we tempted you with Coney Island slides and the Big Dipper. You demanded to be given a go and Mick let you try, again and again, but you kept missing. You were beside yourself. And I took a ball, dropped it into the clowns gaping mouth and I won you a baby doll. You were so happy, so pleased and grateful. Do you remember that?'

'Yeah, I remember now. I called her Michy. I kept her for years,' Haley replied. She looked down at Freddy who continued to feed contentedly. 'Do you remember what you got that trip, what Dad bought you?'

It was Michelle's turn to shake her head.

'He bought you a huge box of Darrell Lea chocolates in the shape of a heart. And made you promise not to share them with anyone. He said they were all for you, from him. They sat on top of the fridge for weeks back home. You ate one a day. I really wanted to try one, but you wouldn't let me. But I saw you offering them to that man who came to fix the washing machine. I was furious.'

They looked at each other. Michelle felt the gap in her daughter's life even after seven years since Mick's death. She reached out and took Haley's hand into her lap, stroked the smooth flesh. She paused and placed her hand alongside her daughter's, elongated her fingers. Her gold wedding ring was tight against the folds of skin; her nails were freshly lacquered vermillion. The young hand beside hers was unadorned and beautifully proportioned.

'I'm getting wrinkly and blotched and fat. Age is catching up with me.'

'Rubbish. You're only sixty-four. Heaps of life left in you.'

'Will you still love me, will you still hold me…?' She sang in a soft mournful voice, the mangled lyrics an earworm of her tangled memory.

'Well Joe does. He adores you. You're lucky.'

'I know. I don't know what's wrong with me today.' She stood up. 'Come on. Freddy's finished his lunch, let's finish ours.'

—

The afternoon progressed with much laughter and merriment, the voices grew louder and the pile of food diminished. Plates of meatballs and braised chicken wings were passed around. Haley noticed the silver platter, laden with kebabs, that had been a wedding gift to Michelle and Joe from her father. She wanted to say something, to bring Mick back, even just for a moment, and her dead brother Frankie too. But she held her thoughts, hid them away from the merriment. She looked at Michelle when Joe refilled the platter. Her mum was shining with joy.

Joe kept up a steady stream of drinks and sizzling delights, proudly announcing each new meaty offering with a butcher's humour. Each dish drew some ribbing, made fun of their increasing girths and ages. He announced, with a flourish of food, his unbridled affection for his wife on their anniversary. Their friends glowed in this affection, making endless toasts to some high point in being middle-aged.

'We're like the beginning of a bloody joke. Look at us!' said Wendy at one stage, gazing about at her friends. 'There was a refugee, a lesbian, a single mum and an old drunk all gathered at a party.'

Her eyes flicked quickly past Freddy. No joke there, she thought.

'Who you calling a drunk?' Harry slurred merrily.

'Well that's a toss-up between you and Nickleass there.'

'And up yours, too sister,' Nicky said, raising her glass with a flourish and peal of laughter. They all grinned in a moment of humorous unity.

In a lull in the conversation Deirdre nudged Harry, who staggered slightly to his feet, pulled a scrap of notepaper out of his pocket, and tapped his glass with a trifle-smeared spoon. The others grew quiet. Freddy lay sleeping gently in Joe's arms, little milk bubbles bursting on his baby lips.

'Folks, I'd like to propose a toast to our wonderful hosts, our most generous of friends, Joe and Michy. I'd like to read you a little verse I copied out from the book in their honour. Hang on a minute.' He patted his pockets furtively, then looked at Deirdre with bleary eyes.

'You must have left them at home dear. Let me.' Deirdre rose and took the paper from him. 'It's not *that* book, don't worry.'

She flattened out the notepaper and held it at arm's length, squinting a little. She read the sentimental poem plainly, and they listened, and the last lines filled the air:

> '*For the locks may bleach, and the cheeks of peach*
> *May be reft of their golden hue;*
> *But mine own sweetheart, I shall love you still,*
> *Just as long as your eyes are blue.*'

There was silence when she finished. Deirdre cleared her throat.

'Err, sorry Joe – Japheth, I know this isn't your heritage but it's Harry's latest favourite poem by Banjo Patterson who's, well you know, *our* poet. He read it to me this morning and I said it reminded me of you both. The way you are together. I dared him to read it to you, but that didn't work, did it? So anyway, here's to our Joe and Michelle.'

She raised her glass and there were cheers all round, and a smattering of slightly embarrassed looks that the wine rescued. Joe smiled and stood up. He pumped up his chest a little and replied.

'I know very well Banjo. He is my heritage too now. But please, humour me in return. A poem from Amir Khusrau, a thirteenth-century Hazara poet, who lived in India but whose father came from my country.

> *'Khusrau darya prem ka, ulti wa ki dhaar,*
> *Jo utra so doob gaya, jo dooba so paar.'*

The sound was like a chant, its emotion raw and foreign. Joe's voice was deep with a rhythmic, mystic tone. His friends had never heard him speak like this in the dozen years they'd known him – he was their local butcher for God's sake! He stopped and let the silence hang, then said in English:

> *'Oh Khusrau, the river of love*
> *Runs in strange directions.*
> *One who jumps into it drowns,*
> *And one who drowns, gets across.'*

He looked across at Michelle, whose eyes had filled with tears and whose fingers were twisting her wedding ring. Around the table the couples touched under the tablecloth; Wendy and Nicky held each other's gaze; Deirdre and Harry looked down at the chaotic remains of the meal that lay scattered about. Haley held her child close to her chest and felt his tiny beating heart through her thin summer dress. Joe sat down quietly and picked up Michelle's hand.

'I am across. I am here with you all,' he said simply.

In the silence a lawnmower started up; it could have been a nightingale.

~

The four older women retired to the kitchen, and Harry and Joe cracked another beer and scraped the charred fat off the BBQ grill. Haley carried a sleeping Freddy into the living room and laid him carefully on the floor, away from the fan that cooled the hot Tablelands summer air. She sat beside him and listened to the conversation that drifted in from the kitchen.

The women, all except Nicky, worked together at a nursing home. They had done so for years and had shared many tales as they changed the bedpans, mopped the floors and kept up the paperwork. Nicky was the new one on the block and Haley could hear her trying to break into the tight threesome as they washed up the plates and dried the dishes.

'What a wonderful meal, Michelle. You went to so much effort. And Joe's so lovely – for a man! So funny and gentle. How did you two meet?'

'Where everyone meets in this town, at the Centrelink office,' said Deirdre with a chuckle. Haley could tell she was still drinking. Sunday afternoon was 'let down' time in Armidale it seemed.

'I worked there after my divorce,' said Michelle. 'Joe came through on a refugee resettlement program.'

'Remember those days we spent in the RSL, comparing bloody exes. The amount of chardonnay we must've drunk. Should've invested in a bottle shop. And all those bloody men who used to offer up their services to "help us get over it!" "Come on luv, we'll show y'a good time".'

'Well you certainly shifted gear, Wendy dear.'

'You two don't know what you're missing.'

'Anyway, Harry and Joe are wonderful men.'

'As long as you don't have to listen to Harry snoring at two in the morning.'

'Nicky snores!'

'Like hell I do.'

The laughter pealed out of the room and wrapped around Haley as she listened. She lay next to Freddy and pulled him close. No-one except her little baby snored next to her at night. Freddy's father had already fucked off, wanted nothing to do with either of them. He left in a blazing storm, accusing Haley of leaving no space for him – with the baby, the PhD, the co-op. But she missed his touch, missed the passion. She felt the loneliness of her thirty-six years come crashing down in the tepid air of northern New South Wales.

Michelle came into the room to find her daughter lying foetal-like on the floor with her baby, the two of them spooned and vulnerable. She watched the way Haley hugged Freddy like a baby doll. Her heart flooded with compassion – for her daughter, her grandson, her husband, her friends. Mick was there, and Frankie too. And in this flood she sensed herself, a tiny speck, washing about like flotsam, hanging on to debris. Joe's words came back to her, and she sank down onto the floor behind Haley and the three of them lay spooning, pod-like. She felt her breath flow deep and expansive, drawing in through the generations that lay there, inhaling the tiny newness of Freddy's life, exhaling the tiredness of her own. And Haley, lying encased, felt herself dissolve and become this breath. She felt, without looking, without touch, sensed without thought or sound, understood without reason, that the rhythm of her life was unfolding, right there, right then.

The tiredness left them all. Never, it seemed, had they been more awake, or felt so present, at peace and had never accepted each other as they did at that moment – lying transcendent on the living room floor to the clatter of crockery and the low deep voices of the men talking cricket – cuddling after lunch.

Catching Yabbies

Every kid should have a creek. Somewhere wild and free and far enough from home for adventures, but close enough to visit easily. Somewhere within range of the dinnertime yell through the flyscreen door. In the city it's where the sewerage and stormwater lines are laid; disused gullies where the necessary wildness has grown back over the concrete inspection holes leaving them moss-covered and protruding like Hollywood boulders, maintaining the illusion. In the bush it's where the cattle can't reach, beyond the blackberry thickets and paddock-edged regrowth. In our case it was down the track that my father had cut with a broad axe as a kid in the Depression, a track for hauling timber to keep the kitchen stove cooking. In the 1960s it was the closest thing to the Wild West any of us could imagine, and we all used to play there, Mick, Bill and me.

It wasn't very large, our creek, but it had flowed across the sedimentary rock for long enough to carve deep pools and

twenty-foot canyons. The water flowed in cool, tumbling cas-
cades. In other places, it dived beneath collapsed sheets of the
escarpment and tunnelled through the rock leaving a day-night
world of glow-worms and unfathomable reaches. On several
occasions we tried to breach those depths, but after that last
time, our father refused to let us go to that part of the creek.
We wouldn't have gone anyway, there was too much shame.

I don't blame it on the creek though. The tales of the Wild
West were always dangerous.

—

Marg had come up from the city. Marg was our only cousin
and at thirteen was self-conscious but equally precocious. She
performed for us boys like you wouldn't believe, lording it over
us in her nascent femininity and city ways that made us feel
inferior – at least she hoped it would. Instead, it made us all act
more feral, and we'd choose to do things just to gross her out:
throw pig shit at each other, squirt steaming milk from the goats'
teats over her clean dresses and generally muck about. But that
last time she visited we weren't all so little. Mick was fifteen,
Bill a year younger, and I was seven. I didn't really have a clue
what was going on most of the time, but I watched. I saw things.

When we picked her up from the train station that summer
Marg had changed. Gone were the dungarees and duffle bag,
wide cheeky smiles and open embraces we were used to from
the previous years, and in their place was a haughty girl with
over-the-shoulder glances, mascara-covered eyelashes, and a
chameleon mood we couldn't fathom. She demanded her own
room, to which my parents quickly assented, so Mick had to

move in with Billy and me. I think that started something off, right from the first day. As the summer progressed she and Mick were at it hammer and tongs, always niggling, arguing and putting each other down. Bill stayed out of it mostly, and I kept trying to get her old self back with childish antics and careless limericks; there was one I kept repeating that seems so prescient now in its childish observations.

> *There was a young maid from the city*
> *Who really was quite pretty.*
> *But Mick stole her dress*
> *The one she liked best*
> *And hid it in his boxing kitty.*

I found the pink dress in Mick's boxing kit in the back of the workshop a few days before that trip to the creek.

—

Why do I dredge this up now, this ancient history of brothers long gone? There are so many horrors and shames in the world that get buried with each death, so many trivial indiscretions and great atrocities and murders. They belong under the ground, discarded, relinquished. What good can it do to dig this one up? What does one more tale tell any of us about ourselves?

My niece came by the other day, with her little boy in tow. And little Freddy said, quick as a flash on entering the door, 'Story Gruncle Jack, when you small,' and I shuffled up out of my chair, grabbed him by the arms and helicoptered him about before plonking him back down on my lap and told him one about catching yabbies in the creek. Up there on the mountain, in the highlands, in that place where I start all my stories for him because he lives in the city and doesn't know this land: any land. Once upon a time. Down by the creek. When the world was young and the big trees only gum-nuts and the joeys poked their heads out from their mothers' pouches, like our little Freddy.

But this one is not for little Freddy; this one is for me. This one is for the sunlight so that I might become a little lighter. It is such a little tale after all. You might shake your head and wonder at the end, like I do; how can such a little tale have weighed down a generation?

—

The morning broke cold, mist hung in the valley but already we could all sense it would be a stinker of a day. We made plans for us kids to spend it down in the creek. Mother packed us a simple lunch of bread and ham, a jar of pickles and instructions to drink up from the creek or we'd 'shrivel like prunes and look like Johnny did when he was born'. She often made that joke, scuffing my hair with affection. The others just groaned: the story of my birth and all the attendant dramas of the workshop delivery were well and truly old news. I had liked to think it was a centrepiece in our family's story, but I see now there are far more central ones that have run across the ages and generations, flowed like lava in the earth, beneath us all.

Mick led the way. Mick always led the way back then, though when it was only Billy and I we managed easy enough. Down the slope we thundered, with Marg yelling 'wait up' in echo of a receding call from my father to 'look out for your cousin, boys,' which we studiously ignored. Once past the rusted barbed wire fence, where the goats could no longer reach, the bush grew beautiful again. I loved that bush. On quiet days Billy and I would lie in the shade of the old white gums on a carpet of wallaby grass and make whistles with juvenile eucalypt leaves, imitating the kites that wheeled about on the pasture verge looking for rabbits and mice. Lower down, as the shade grew deeper and the moisture fought off the summer heat, the tree ferns flourished and it was there that the real tales of our childhood were created. The glades gave a muted light that curtained a multitude of mysteries, a dragon's den, an Indian hideout. Away from the brightness of the pasture and the upper slopes near the house, we could invent almost anything: and we did.

'There's a red-bellied black snake living in that hole, Marg. You'd better be careful.'

'The leeches here have special saliva. Your blood will flow forever. You'll bleed to death!'

Marg could see it was mostly bullshit, but she was nervous enough that she picked her way with extra caution over the rotting logs and slippery boulders. Still, she had a few of her own; she was, after all, a Ferguson.

'Did you know there is a velvet worm found in New England that has a cranial phallus? I wonder if they named it after you lot?'

'Look, perhaps this is it,' she'd say, holding up a fat, grotesque earthworm the size of her little finger. Or another time, a pale flaccid witchetty grub that the cockatoos had missed when they'd shredded the wattle.

But the antics were fairly mild on that warming summer's day as we headed for the rock pool. Mick was quieter than usual, and he kept slowing to let Marg catch up. She was more ungainly at rock-hopping this trip and in her clumsiness she'd reach out for him, grabbing his arm and falling against him. He seemed to like the chance to show off his strength, hauling her up and over logjams and snags that Billy and I simply walked around. Then he'd revert to his old form and throw an insult her way that she'd batter back.

'They might teach you Latin in the city, but at least we can walk.'

'Yes, such a newfound skill for the recently evolved. It gets passé after a while and we in the city invented cars. You should try them one day, Mr Gorilla.'

Eventually we got to the largest pool in the creek, the one fed in part by the water pouring through the tunnel in the rock. At this time of the year the water was only a trickle, and the narrow cavity beckoned. Twenty feet up the cliff face another rivulet fell the full height of the waterfall. It was our habit to leap off this rock shelf into the cool water. Bill was the best by far, fearless in his summersaults and star jumps. Mick just plunged down, graceless but powerful, exploding into the pool with a force that sent the spray arching up like whale spouts. At certain times and angles rainbows would appear in the vapour, and Billy and I would egg him on to do it again so we could marvel at the colours. Mick always thought we were admiring his bombs. My jumps were far less bold. I still had to work up the courage to jump from the top, making do with a leap from a halfway rock shelf that I alone could scramble to, squeezing under algae-covered, slippery rocks and hanging finger ferns. I usually compensated with a yell like a banshee warrior, though my brothers called it the squeal of a stuck pig.

When we got to the pool this time I stripped off and jumped

straight in, diving down to see if there were any yabbies before the others got in and clouded the water or scared them off. But when I surfaced empty-handed and looked back, the three of them were standing on the shore just watching me. Even though I was a few yards away, I could sense the uncertainty and awkwardness between them. Marg stood with her arms tightly folded, her head held high and her hair falling halfway down the back of her firmly-in-place white dress. She had a look of magisterial nonchalance mixed with hyper-alertness. Mick had paused with his shirt off, stuck in a half-strutting muscle-man pose. Bill, fully dressed, just looked goofy: eyes down, feet shuffling, breathing like he was sucking up the static of a summer thunderstorm.

Marg broke the spell.

'I didn't bring any swimmers,' she said.

We all just looked at her. I hadn't even thought about it.

'Go in your undies,' Bill replied. 'Mick and I will too.'

'Or we could all go nude like we always have,' Mick said, dropping his t-shirt and reaching for his daks.

'Mick!' Bill put his hand on our brother's arm. 'She doesn't want to.'

'Well if Johnny can, I am.'

'Then I won't swim,' Marg replied.

She started walking away around the pool's edge to the shady side, her comment stopping Mick in mid-strip.

I swam back to the shore where I'd dumped my clothes and put on my undies, then splashed over to Marg as she squatted by the water's edge scribbling patterns in the sandy shoreline with a stick.

'Do you want to look for yabbies?' I asked her.

She didn't look up or acknowledge me. I waded over to where the pool drained back into the creek. The yabbies were often gathered there, filtering tiny critters and detritus that got swept up in the flow.

—

It must have been half an hour before Marg finally came back into the sun. Mick and Bill had stripped to their boxers and were tomfooling in the shallows, Bill standing on Mick's shoulders, getting him to wade up to his chest and then doing backflips into the depths. The ripples from his tumbles washed the rocks where I searched, but the water seemed to darken the stone for only a moment. The heat of the day was rising; even coming from the shade I could see that Marg was sweating. Out of the corner of my eye I watched her unzip her dress and walk tentatively but gracefully into the cool water. Mick and Bill watched too. In her small bra and knickers her body shape was on full display, and everyone knew it. The swell of her hips was shrouded in pretty frills of white, and there was a woman-ness to her breasts that Mick couldn't take his eyes off. She swam out into the centre of the pool and then duck-dived down and disappeared under the surface leaving only the smallest of ripples. We peered into the shimmering surface, shielded our eyes from the glare of the reflecting sun, but none of us could make out where she'd gone.

The moment dragged on. It was too long for her breath. Bill swam to where she'd dived, his head swivelling this way and that, searching about, anxious. Still the water reflected only the dazzling blue sky and the dark rock of the cliff face.

'Can ya see her?'

'No. You?'

'Fuck. Where is she?'

Then Mick gave a yell and fell forward. Up popped Marg, grinning and wet and laughing in great lung-fulls of gasping breath. Mick coyly pulled up his underpants below the waterline.

We all mucked about after that, reverting to the creek games of previous years, and then taking time out to lie under the waterfall's beating hammer till we couldn't stand the thumping anymore. After lunch we sunbaked in the shade of the pittosporum and listened to the creek sounds. The waterfall played slapping rhythms on the pool surface that we each took as our own song, and in the somnolence of that summer's day, it was playful and serene. Above the water stories, the cicadas twirled and whirled and keep up a drone of constant sharpness. Over by the rock face, the black hole of the tunnel beckoned.

Mick was the first to mention the tunnel, challenging the rest of us to a dare. Who would go into the tunnel, right in, and see if they could climb up to the top, to where the water plummeted in through a crack in the creek bed? He and Bill had tried years before but had got beaten by some log jams and the force of the water pushing down. Or so they said. I'd gone in once too, the previous summer, and seen the glow-worms and felt where the tunnel suddenly dropped and opened out, part of the rock shelf undermined. But I'd stopped there. I couldn't grab onto anything to climb; the walls were cold and wet and smooth. It was too dark.

This year the creek was at the lowest it had been in ages. The long dry spell had turned the pastures to crackling brown early, and the trees were shedding leaves and bark like I'd never seen.

The creek, though still flowing, had shrunk away from the crack in the bedrock and tracked a lower path over the cliff face, leaving the tunnel mostly dry. The challenge had new possibilities.

Marg was the first to respond, still smarting a little from Mick's comments earlier.

'I'll lead, Micky boy,' she taunted. 'Follow if you dare.'

She strutted off and climbed with ease the low rock shelf to the tunnel's entrance. Mick grinned and followed, watching her every move. Billy and I shrugged and dived back into the pool: it wasn't our game. Anyway, I hoped the yabbies might have appeared in our absence from the water over lunch, tricked by the temporary stillness. But even though we weren't going into the tunnel and it wasn't our game, we too, were alive to the dare.

—

I've not thought about this story for a long time, but it is here now, shuffling its way along sluggish neurons. The 'brothers grim' I call my siblings, as they appear and disappear from memory. So many moments play out, decades later, with a different cast, the script still raw, but the players transposed. In the background were our parents, but it was us brothers that tarmacked the road. What I'm hoping is that the brilliance of the summer sunshine will blister the bitumen and leave enough pockmarks in the tales to shred their path. I don't trust forgetting, it has a nasty habit of resurfacing. And of all the jobs that are in the hell realms, working on the hot bitumen road gang with boiling tar ingrained in the flesh is the one I fear. And still, this is such a little tale.

It was Marg's scream we heard first, echoing out of the tunnel, chilling us even on that most sweltering of days. Billy and I thrashed through the water to the tunnel's entrance. There were more yells, Mick's and Marg's voices tangled and frightening; we couldn't make any sense of them. Bill started to crawl in, but he was waylaid almost immediately by Marg who burst, hot and angry, out of the mouth of the tunnel, mud splattered on her face. Her hair was streaked with slime. She pushed past Bill and ran for her clothes on the beach. I looked down and saw the blood on the inside of her legs and her knickers torn and hanging. She grabbed her dress and disappeared into the bush before we could say a word, but not before Mick appeared at the tunnel entrance yelling after her.

'What happened? Bill asked, his voice tense and blaming.

'Fuck knows,' Mick replied. 'We reached the drop where we could stand and I was guiding her up to that ledge on the right. All of a sudden she was thrashing against me, screaming, and then pissed off out the tunnel.'

'That's it?' I asked, looking at Bill. 'She was bleeding. Her undies were torn.'

'What? I swear I didn't touch her.'

Bill was shaking his head and starting off through the bush after Marg.

'Bullshit, Mick,' he said, throwing the comment over his shoulder.

I looked at Mick and could see he was shocked, but also angry, his face red. Then he too stormed across the shallows, grabbed his clothes and followed Bill into the bush.

⌒

I don't know why I never told them what I saw next. I didn't know what was going on and wasn't sure what it meant. But as I walked slowly to where my clothes were, something made me turn back and look at the tunnel, and that's when I saw the goanna. At least I think that's what I saw. A fleeting glimpse of what looked like a tail and splayed back legs: slipping beneath the water. I stared for a long time, searched all across the pool's surface, but nothing appeared beneath the reflection of endless blue.

⌒

'Look, Grunckle Jack!'

Freddy held out his hand and revealed a small black beetle. It crawled about his palm, but as it got near the edge, he'd push it gently back into the centre of his hand.

'Tickles,' he said.

'Where'd you find it, little man?'

'Under tree. He my pet.'

'Do you think he's hungry? Or thirsty? Maybe he's missing his family. Perhaps you should let him go?'

Freddy looked up at me with large serious eyes.

'Yes. Take him back. See where he lives?'

We walked out to the wilder part of the garden where the branches of the blue gum lay tumbled and rotting and the leaf litter was thick and moist. Freddy gently placed his small hand down among the leaves, and this time, let the beetle crawl off the edge. We watched as it struggled across some twigs and dried leaves in the sunlight, and then breathed a little collective sigh as it crawled out of sight under a nondescript brown leaf.

'What Grandpa like, Gruncle Jack? Tell me Grandpa Mick story.'

'What do you imagine he was like, Freddy? Perhaps you can tell me a story.'

On the Haiku Trail to Nowhere

2027

I BUILT A HUT UP on Grey Mountain – away from it all, you might say. I prefer to say 'in amidst it all' if anybody ever challenges me, but they rarely do nowadays. They said I was crazy when I started in my mid-sixties lugging sheets of iron up the slopes. They felt I should have been enjoying my retirement – playing golf, Winnebagoing about the countryside, relaxing. But playing Sherpa suited me; a curling back while moving on, building something even as I tried to let go of everything else. Others have done it in style; Milarepa, the poet saint of Tibet, in the eleventh century thrice built a great stone tower only to destroy it each time, such was his practice. The fourth stayed up. I'll settle for one small hut: my energy is waning.

If there had been a cave I might have simply moved in, but I couldn't find one. The steep southern slopes of sassafras and myrtle are tangled and dark. Filamentous ferns cling to cliff faces. Lots is hidden still. My little rock shelter has dry-stone walls, a tin roof, a single glass window and a slab door. It's up high: I can see the ocean, other islands and the craggy mountains of the Southern Ranges. Adamsons Peak is snow-covered in winter.

I carried all the tools back down when I'd finished. The hut will last long enough before it falls apart and rots away. We might do it together.

I live in the hut most days now, an hour's walk up an intermittent track – route really – from the wooden shack at the roadhead that is also home. It is hard to imagine living anywhere else. I like living in these interstices where the paths stop and we step into nowhere. Don't get me wrong, I have visitors. I'm not really a hermit. Freddy and Haley are the most welcome. Occasionally her other boy, Daniel – the one that was let go of, only to be found. The odd bushwalker rolls up every now and then. Stonehouse is the most frequent visitor and he's been dead nearly 700 years.

It is bleak in winter. There is ice on the oxbow of the creek and on the tarns, and when it snows the path to the dunny is slippery and needs all my attention. My bones lock up if I sit too long on the long-drop, gazing at the Southern Ocean with the winds of Antarctica leaking in through the vertical boards; they tell me to attend with haste. The Poles are still cold, even as they melt.

I look east, towards the sunrise. I am east: of the ancient histories of Europe that I once taught, further east than the stories of Asia I learnt. Now, I see the sun rising up from the ocean like the birth that it is, triumphant from amniotic waters, searing and alive. Shining onto this land every day of my birth, a place so particular few can find it among the scree slopes of ice-cracked boulders and burnt-out stags of mountain ash from other flames, decades before.

Of course death is near. When is it not?

—

I'm still writing, carefully now. The paper on which my rheumatic hand marks like some scribbly gum larvae is precious, though 'precious' is perhaps too sacred a word for the poems that land there. Moments put down, my koans answered in a fleeting gesture of surprise at anything so captured in words. Worrying about a thought is like collecting firewood when the ridge is ablaze.

Still, my ego wonders about the death poem that will rise. Years ago I read brother Mick's final letter with some surprise – and lots of sadness. That he got so close only to miss by a mile. Haley thought he'd found peace: with the bees, the bush, with her. It looked like renunciation. What was he thinking, then, in that chaos of cancer, in that last breath? Did he really imagine, as he said in the letter, that the destruction of his body, of the house, of the stories – the *stuff* – of his life, would free his family, his lovers, would free *us*? Or himself? Did he think *he* could wipe out the connections by such destruction? That Haley would be able to let go when she was pushed so hard? Oh Mick, such foolish wisdom.

Maybe, later, something simpler was left just before the flames consumed him. Perhaps he wrote a note in his mind, without a reader to discern, a brother to compete, the forgiveness of a daughter to implore. Maybe he'd made peace by then. I hope so.

In moments of madness I try on death poems. I can remember those of others. Stonehouse's sits sublime, but then he had an audience of fourteenth-century Chinese monks to applaud, and reprint the poem, when he'd flung down his final pen:

> *corpses don't stink in the mountains*
> *there's no need to bury them deep*
> *I might not have the fire of samadhi*
> *but enough wood to end this family line*

My family is also eaten; the devils here scrounge all our souls. I hear them at night on the bush track, fighting over carrion with snarling shrieks and coughing growls; at least they won't need to bring up an undertaker for me.

~

Stonehouse and I sat together again last night. I read his poems and he laughed at mine.

'Why write?' he asked.

Pointing to the stringybark beam I had so roughly hewn from gale-felled timber, he traced the path of an insect borer that had eaten out the sapwood.

'See,' he said. 'It ate and grew fat, broadened its path and left its mark. Metamorphosed. We can trace its movements, wonder at its appetite, watch its growth, but do you think of it, our little borer taken flight? Or just see its scribbles? What makes you think your life will be remembered even if your poems are?'

I smile at his questions, he who visits me in the clouds on Grey Mountain and who lingers only occasionally in the mist.

We have grown accustomed to each other. I know he isn't real and he knows I'm not. Our clothes are tattered; his robe's sky-patched. We get along fine, two failed hermits yarning away our days, weaving stories from the curlicues of condensation that float on mountaintops.

I spill more wine over his cup. He laughs and scoops up the sodden dirt and pours it back in.

'This isn't milk,' he says, grinning. 'Besides, I need the roughage: you doubt me!

> *'Trying to become a buddha is easy*
> *but ending delusion is hard*
> *how many frosty moonlit nights*
> *have I sat and felt the cold before dawn'*

But all my family aren't dust; only the dead are gone. Freddy came to the shack the other day, blew the old radong that I keep by the back door, just for him and Haley. The sounds reverberated up the valley and soon brought me down. Calling the dead from their graves – my little joke – 'cause I think the gods around here aren't listening for a monastic awakening but are mighty busy with the valley folk fighting each other over plastic dreams. Fighting the Dreaming Wars for a monetary awakening instead.

The first time Freddy saw the radong on my return from the east I told him it was a gift from Tibet. From the steppes south-west of the Gobi Desert, where there were wars of another kind, and where there were warriors like him only they didn't see half as much as his kind eyes. Nor hear the music that he found and shared with me. The radong was taller than he was, and he blew into it and the sound came out loud and clear from the fluted trumpet and the laughter that came from Freddy rang with the echo. Together the sounds chased each other right around the valley, up over the mountain and came back as a note of purity I still smile to hear. A forest raven matched it, then a currawong, and later, when he was asleep in his mother's arms as we sat by the fire drinking wine and catching up on other tales, I swear the mopoke picked up the same note. Haley and I looked at each other and smiled. Her Buddha boy for whom we all suffered in expectation was already singing with the stars and we could only shake our heads in wonderment at his sound.

We walk a lot, Freddy and I. On the days when he sleeps over in the shack we go on expeditions across the mountain. I show him my discoveries and he shows me his: leaves that float like wind horses off the rocky crags, the tunnel of a pademelon pad that threads away into the bush and only a nimble boy can follow. The splash of white guano under a roosting branch where the bones tell us an eagle has sat feeding above. Bones we make clap sticks from, in celebration of the timbre of the dead, because we can, because we have no need for sorrow or shame or righteous action: an old man and his greatly enabled great-nephew, making thunderclaps with our bones. Maybe Freddy will beat the devils to mine. I hope his tears will be fleeting.

—

But most days it is sparser.

Most days, like today, I sit alone, stilling the mind. Sound is made by the wind through me, carrying my thoughts away before I follow them, chasing echoes. These are the days when

I am on the Haiku trail to Nowhere. When the wandering is on folded knees, and the dolerite, just here, is a fraction more worn.

I fail often. My mind wanders. Jessie, my old flame, dances in my mind still, though more freely now. At times she plays on the wind with me, and I dance up there on the rocky shelf that extols the virtue of heights below the summit. My desire and longing I try and cast in the mind's mirror as a luminous deity of love with one thousand arms and a myriad of manifestations. Facing east, my hands open in a new mudra and this time the vessel that is shaped holds everything in the swirling mountain air. My tears are droplets of that same mist coalescing on a face that warms by its very life the waters within and without. My blood is that of the trees and earth alike.

—

I'm not alone really. My worlds are melding: dreams manifest, expectations disappoint. Searching for perfection, I keep stubbing my toes like a child teetering on new ground. The blood brings me back. I'm living in a mandala where the rooms are without walls now.

Others *do* accompany me. I became aware of them years ago. Slowly, almost imperceptibly, I felt something on the periphery. I started muttering strange words to myself, made-up words that stuck on my tongue and remained there like a memory of a new–old language. Words born of the earth, of the calls of the birds and the rasping of trees. The thump of the pademelons. The freeze–thaw grating of rocks.

Beyond words, an otherness approached. At night, lights jiggled where no light should have been: crazy jack-o-lanterns among the trees. On the rocky eyrie where I could survey the whole valley, the feelings were strongest. We are never alone if we are not lonely, but in the darkness, the blackness, the presence resisted my gaze.

At first I was self-conscious. How was I meant to act with this history, the terrible things that have happened here? I picked up the mudstone flakes from the valley floor that were full of fossils; they made no sound. I felt the pull of oceans without the fear of drowning. I sensed about me figures that had sat on that rock and worn the grey dolerite smooth with deep shadows. A hand on the trunk of that gnarled snow gum, watching the way the clouds played on distant peaks. People whose Country I was standing on, waiting to see what I would do.

I sat on the ground.

The cold rock beneath me held me as I waited for something to manifest: anything. To hear the stories of these people, to hear what I should do, but around me the presence just continued to be, and nothing happened.

But it did. I just didn't see it at first. Now I am growing here: in company.

—

I work in the little garden each day now, mumbling metaphysics to Stonehouse, and watching lines of ants carrying quartzite crystals up from caverns deep beneath my blade. Up the valley a tractor's drone is carried on a southerly wind. Sweat pours down my arms and makes damp imprints on the hoe's smooth and sun-bleached handle: bone white. The weeds are few, little pink *Centaurium* scattered like mythical markings. Eventually what

rises is not of my making but something far more unexpected –
flowers! Though I plant a crop in the hope of a harvest, today's
work seems enough for today. I breathe in steady rhythm as
I sow. From the eyrie the black snake of tarmac is threaded with
other fleeting ants. The wedge-tailed eagles fly afternoons when
the thermals are rising, covering huge distances with grace and
ease and soaring home each evening above me as I sit at sunset.

—

Days pass. I hear the call reverberating up the valley and I cooee
Freddy up the slope. We greet each other on the rocky ledge
by the hut. We have sung each other again – the lines connect.

'Grunkle,' Freddy says.

His face is beaming, the sweat falls freely from his forehead.

'Hey kid. Glad to see you're still dancing.'

He grins and gives a little jig on the spot, the music alive in
him. He's almost as tall as me; I'm bending as he grows.

Years ago when I left the city I left him too. I left not because
of the noise of garbage trucks and street sweepers, lawn mowers
and leaf blowers, but of what I couldn't hear and see. Beyond
my senses the city had seeped into me and tightened my very
cells. Electrified my body so that I had become immune to too
much; overstimulated, I had shut down. I couldn't hear Freddy's
song, nor that of the stars that only shone there with a fraction
of their age, nor see the passage of our own sun as fleeting
clouds broke up its cadence. The solar winds were silenced but
I knew there was a symphony, I had heard it in the mountains.
So I came further south to dwell upon these slopes in quietude,
and write my poems.

But Freddy is not to be abandoned, and Haley still battles her demons and seeks a life more sensuous than mine. Mid-life in a mad rush she's made her mark. Motherhood has touched her twice and those of us from the village diaspora will raise them both, it seems.

'Poem, Grunkle?' Freddy asks, breaking my reverie.

His voice is still high though the cuffs of his old worn shirt barely reach his wrists. He must have missed a beat when buttoning up, one side's askew; maybe it was jazz. Snot hangs from his nose.

I give him an old haiku, just to tease.

> *Falling off the world*
> *Fishermen ply their bleak trade*
> *Zen hooks are empty!*

I feel his eyes on me. They moisten a little and I feel – ashamed. The poem is too full. He doesn't know where to go with it. Somewhere Stonehouse is shaking his head. It's not that Freddy's only a boy, or is different. It's that the image belongs elsewhere. I start anew.

'Let's walk, Freddy.'

'Where?'

'Where do you want to go?'

'Rock-hopper penguin. To Mum.'

But he says it with a gleam now. I'm already forgiven – with laughter. He's my teacher, my guru – it's humbling.

We head on down the slope to where the scree field is, and as the sun warms our backs, we crazy hop from boulder to boulder.

'Slow man, Grunkle,' yells Freddy, already yards ahead of me.

My joints are aching. He's heavy on his feet but quick. He leaps from boulder to boulder with his own grace, each landing determined and focused, childlike. Suddenly he stops. I see him slowly sit on a rock and reach down. By the time I get to him he's totally immersed in whatever it is that his broad back is blocking from my sight. He ignores me.

'What is it Freddy? What have you found?'

He holds his right hand up slowly. Stop.

I peer over his shoulder and my ragged breath catches. Everything stops – the mountain, the forest, the sun: frozen, rigid. Sliding over his feet is a metre-long tiger snake. Its tongue flicks, its head sways. Freddy's left palm is open on the ground before it. The adrenaline pounds in me, but I can't move. I dare not. I watch as the snake glides onto Freddy's palm. He gently lowers his other hand onto its back, his fingers spread wide. As the snake slides forward its yellow stripes flicker beneath Freddy's bar-straight fingers. The boy and the tiger snake appear to stroke each other. The cage is open.

There's nothing I can do. Any movement may startle the snake. My heart races and I take tiny breaths, trying to be as still as Freddy. I can hear the snake's skin rasp against the lichen on the rock. Its head goes back into a cooler crevasse between the boulders. I feel my shoulders loosen as the narrow tail finally leaves Freddy's palm.

We don't say anything, but I'm trembling. We continue to watch as the snake winds through the shadows, its tongue still flickering. Its low flat head rises and falls as it scents its way ahead. Only when it is a few metres away do I fully breathe. The sound of my exhalation is loud in the stillness.

Holy shit. I feel my anger surge.

Freddy turns to look at me, smiling broadly, the joy shining in his eyes.

There is nothing I can say. He is looking at my fear and smiling it away.

—

When we get to the shack and Freddy's already telling his mother excitedly what happened, I write:

Summer trails
scree rock hopping
shadows move

because Freddy has shown me the world. Again.

—

That evening, as his mother rests in the shack from her own stresses, I recite other poems to him. Poems I write to catch a single day. Sitting in the cooling air, we wander through my weeks and months on the haiku trail, and he sings his accompaniments.

I stop
currawong calls stop
we listen

'crawa cawa, crackawa, boom bah, ahhhh ...'

roof scratching
rank rat shit
dusk swallows

'shirka sirk boom bah, scratchy ratchi, woo haaa…'

Eventually he falls asleep as the trail fades, buried under the pure white snow of months ago.

Fresh snow
the trail widens
what now?

As I lie in the dark I can hear the gentle sounds of Freddy's and Haley's breathing in the other room. The air is cool through the open window. Tonight it carries the sounds of masked owls.

⁓

The morning breaks clear and quickly warms. When Haley and Freddy have packed the car and gone, I work the garden.

intellect fades
hoeing loves flowers
poems grow

summer winds
ridge gaze sniffing
tomatoes ripen

~

I walk up through the scree slope to the hut – my eyes alert – and gaze out, this time to the north. There is smoke on the horizon today, and the wind blows from the north in gusts that lift the dried leaves and twigs in unsettling aerial eddies. The animals are moving. I can hear them thumping in the bush in nervous motion. The birds have already flown, the yellow-tailed black cockatoos careering off the mountain, not heralding rain, but ahead of the raining ash that has started to fall. The wind dancers are charred, and a pigmy possum sits nervously by the hut tarn, watching me watching him watching me. I place an ark stone for him out in the shallow water.

Suddenly it is all so quick.

The embers rain down. I can smell the wool of my meditation shawl singeing as I pull it over my head. Pen in hand, I sit outside the hut with the wind behind me looking south. There is no place to flee on this day of creaking bones and a life long-lived. Fire is the present.

The swirling air thickens, a curling of all forms that disappear in acrid smoke and time itself is turning in. I cough, and choke, haul the searing air into my lungs that burn, burn, burn. I cannot see. I cannot breathe. The heat shreds me, the smoke suffocating, cloying, blistering.

There is no air to even scream.

And then the pain, so intense, stops.

The heat: stops.

The beat: stops.

~

A flame intense, a firestorm roars. The vortex sucks the very marrow from the bones. The family that has gone before and those still to come, join. The cycle turns like a ship's wheel that has thrown all pilots and helmsmen and is spinning free. It casts across the divide so suddenly bridged, revealing how I–he–we lived.

All the anger and fear and loathing and shame,

and love and longing and grasping and blame.

This swirling, whirling, curling, world of light and fire brings the brothers of youth who never left. We have journeyed the cycle of all beings, sought shelter in the delusions of the mind.

Till thought ceases.

Sensations pure rise from the heat
rhythms play out on the trail,
no print is left for the final word
which falls, in a single luminous drop,
from sky caverns measureless to man.

Bodies float in fleeting glimpses
life's memory has turned into
the briefest of all possible sounds.
A primordial mantra
spins in endless depths and folds
into this feeling that is given out
without a line to reel it in, or grasp it back,
or ask for more,
but only offered up
in the certitude that,

when the final flame
bursts through the mind to fall
and end suffering
love
will the end
be

pen snaps
ink blot widens
a poem!

The Children of the
Underworld

*Remember these teachings, remember the clear light, the
pure bright shining white light of your own nature. It is
deathless.*

The Tibetan Book of the Dead

FRANKIE LAY AT THE BOTTOM of the pool, looking up at the liquid
orb of the moon. At the edge of the pool, down at the shallow
end with her pale feet dislocated by the mirror surface, sat a
crying Simone. She cradled a formless body in her shaking arms
as another in turn sat on her shoulder and with the stillest of
hearts, watched it all.

A ship's horn sounded in the distance and the noise sent
ripples across the water, breaking the glassy surface. Over the
railing, Jessie watched the reflected line of each single lighthouse
flash, but the period was irregular and impossible to count. The
lighthouse was on a reef, bell-tower-like, and unattainable, so
far from the shore.

Mick paddled the life raft across the pool. He was never going to make it, and anyway, there was already the thumping sound of Chinook helicopters laden with the Valkyries. Bill's enraged yell from the open door behind machine gun flashes was inaudible. But the fight was already over. John's hands were empty of any pen, of anything. The dead were being counted and bundled away in body bags.

On the water a shimmering remained and the surface tension held up more than just the weight of reflected sorrow. The pinpoints of starlight flickered and shifted, doppler red and blue; their names the names of the 'characters' – now so familiar but still uncertain – that shone like constellations swirling around each other and an arbitrary label. The moon hovered bright, levitating miraculously above the world.

—

Simone and Frankie met for a moment, briefly, like a flash of lightning. There was so much that was improbable, it wasn't just the light. In the great timeless cycle of death and rebirth, of samsara, the child and the parent – all children, all parents – become each other.

'Did you forget you couldn't swim?'

'Did you? Is that why you fell in love again? You forgot how dangerous the rip was?'

'What do you know about love? You're too young.'

'Really? What's too young for love? My father caught me from my mother's womb.'

'Surely a body or two should have fallen first. A broken heart or two. A burial. Don't you think so, Bill?'

'Keep me out of this. What would I know? But bodies – I've seen plenty. We all have, if we care to remember them. Do you think that makes me an expert lover?'

'It was hot. I needed to cool off. To get away – in the end.'

'Did you? Get away I mean. Listen – the ship's still sounding. It must be deafening for you. Look – the moon is still murky, milky, is it a mirage?'

'That's your tears, not the moon. Do you still love him?'

'Who?'

—

Simone could have let it go sooner, nothing really prevented her, but she didn't. She kept it all: the letters, the photos, the gifts. His scent she bottled, and then was afraid to open the bottle lest she lose it, so instead she imagined his smell, staring at the empty bottle. The first few anniversaries of their meeting she lay awake, hoping. What began with so much joy imprisoned her with so much suffering. Was this still love? The years folded on top of each other to form a blanket too thick to breathe beneath, yet even suffocating, she held on. The warmth was deceiving.

Frankie swam towards her. Who was he, really? It was a child she yearned for, someone to love. Her empty arms shook uncontrollably, and her womb felt hard and thick.

Frankie saw her as an angel. He swam to the surface overcome with joy.

—

She wasn't sure whether she was dead or not. Her diary filled with stories of a broken heart, so perhaps she was. But then the breeze blew offshore from the hot dry interior and she felt the sweat hang from her lips and the moisture was real enough. Her womb pulsed inside her, but that felt a phantom yearning and she willed herself in charge of it. Anger filled that vessel instead. She hated the pity she felt for herself. She promised never to open her heart to another man. She cradled her arms around the unborn child that never was and still her tears fell. The years rolled on relentless.

How is it that some are never blessed in love? Or when the blessing comes, it is as fleeting as a pontifical hand. She had no faith left in love and the breeze blew hotter and her lips tightened and thinned and her body shrunk away from the breath of a man.

The baby drained away with the bathwater. Bitterness lined the rim. It didn't have to be this way.

—

She entered Mick's dreams like a light beam: a god ray after a distant storm. The energy was manifest; she still walked the shores of his wakening. But the flames were even brighter.

—

The crackling sound of the fire competed with the screaming, but he couldn't tell whose it was, it might have been his own, or simply the sounds of green wood venting steam. Right up to that last moment Mick felt sure he'd be fine, felt sure the sheer horror of it all was already known. The apocalypse – he'd imagined it many a day. But it wasn't the same. He was still too weighed down for that last leap. Renunciation? He destroyed what he couldn't let go of. Freedom remained elusive. Around him it all crumbled, and the smoke gave way to demons.

⁓

Simone wasn't dead. Love rescued her, and her womb filled with life and a little boy was born and she named him Mick: foolishly. The years rolled on and little by little things got lost in house moves and memory blackouts – a shoebox gone walkabout, a wooden box shunted to the sloping attic corner. Eventually even the name lost its legacy and all that Micky boy knew was the sing-song sound of his name being yelled out from the sidelines by his wildly passionate mother and burly builder dad and like every child he simply craved the love of the centre, however small the circle.

You see: a happy ending can be found. Just let go.

In the attic the box with dovetailed corners shimmered in the uncertainty of endings. Eventually we have to grow up, even if it takes lifetimes. But can we keep alive beauty? Playfulness? Laughter?

⁓

Pete's time was the briefest, the most transcendent. They didn't try to call him back, though their tears were sorrowful and his heart the most open. Not the youngest, for their hearts returned the same age in death, but the most raw in the best use of the word: flesh, fresh, bloody, clean, and pure.

How could someone so small have such a big heart? His mind infused it with love. They all felt it when they lowered him into the ground, and he, in turn, felt their love and though they wailed later, right then, he let them go. His presence had brought more joy into the world. It was fleeting, and quiet, and the pure light shone all around. The wattle was brilliant in shining yellow and the spring air the deepest blue. His little–great heart filled with compassion, and he let them go and spun away into that intense luminous yellow light. Such a brief time, but sufficient: too short to gather the baggage of birth, long enough to loosen that last vestige of attachment. Some noticed the signs. A rainbow appeared without the cry of black cockatoos and the air was dry away from the tears. His tiny hands uncurled by themselves beneath the cloth and casket lid. A light shone through the shroud.

—

'There was something far too poetic about leaving on a rainbow. But being called a hippie never troubled me. I always took it as a compliment; so often it was cloaked in jealousy.'

Jessie and John were talking again, timelessly now.

'They blew it up in the end, didn't they? The Rainbow I mean.'

'Don't they always?'

'Still, it could be worn as its own cloak of subterfuge. Hiding in a rainbow. But it isn't really the clothes, is it? Try wearing a suit at a campfire, a rainbow scarf on Wall Street, a pair of Speedos at the nudist beach. Ever wondered why Lady Jane Beach was renamed Lady Bay; there's even a uniform for the naked it seems.'

'Huh?'

'You tried to hold onto the rainbow! After he died. You built something else, a craven image. Tough campaigner. Peace laced with anger … at yourself.'

'Crap. That's your projection.'

'Were the rocks that invisible that you didn't take heed of them? How bright do you need the bloody light to be?'

'Fuck off. We all crash. Get shipwrecked sometime. Isn't that the point? To be humbled, to let go of the ego. To know how beauty fades and strength diminishes.'

'Beauty doesn't fade, only our eyes. I saw the most sublime sunrise from Grey Mountain. Didn't you see it?'

'The fog was too thick. That's why they kept sounding the horn.'

'How's your hearing?'

'Do you know what the sound of love is?'

John was silent as the koan blew through him.

—

Jessie kept sailing. Her albatross hung around her neck and time just left her body sagging under the weight. Old age had her still standing on the deck, hanging onto the railing, but the vessel was always moored alongside a disused wharf in San Francisco. She'd bought an old wooden ketch with peeling varnish and splintered spars, thought to restore it but time had just got away. The fishermen used to leave fish for her and her cats, fish they would otherwise have thrown back. Dickens meets Coleridge on another continent's shore – the new world – yet even there the empty wharves were already laden with too many memories, and poverty clung to her like the fog. Her rainbow flag still fluttered from a mast bereft of rigging but proudly erect; the boat swayed a little on the tide and the wash of container ships passing further out in the bay. She would struggle up from below deck at sunset, hauling her tired body to watch the city lights come on and listen to the voices that carried across the water. With all the traffic the bay was never still and she never did see her reflection again and anyway, her eyesight was milky with cataracts. But pleasure was still there in the evening glow of the red and green channel markers and the passing cabin lights of ferries, freighters and passenger ships heading out under the golden arc of the bridge.

By her bunk was a little shrine with that photograph of her stillborn child from more than half a century before, and as she prepared for bed each evening in the narrow cabin, she would light a single incense stick and wish him well on his way.

Eventually she realised Pete was all around her in that luminous yellow light that came up each morning and it was no longer sadness she was keeping there by the bed; the smell of memory became the smell of the sublime even as it mixed with the odour of her own decay. Happiness takes so many forms; the spectrum of white light is infinite.

⁓

It was blue, Frankie's light. He floated towards, through, the almost translucent blue. The angel had gone, the cloying crushing suffocating sensation had left too, and the wailing had long gone silent. What was he meant to know, to feel, to understand? He'd already forgotten their names, even as he felt them trying to haul him back – and he wanted to go back. He could feel his sister's guilt, and he wanted to tell her it was alright. He wanted to snuggle back into her arms, unsay the unkind words, and give her back her night of womanhood that he'd stolen with his sinking. Swamped with his suffocation. Downed with his drowning. It wasn't his fault, he tried to say, screamed at them, cried with them, but the light burned him up and the horror was too strong.

They came at him with gnashing teeth, their kisses transformed into snarling hungry bites that feasted on his body, tore at his flesh. From the cold freezing depths of the water he was hauled into the flames. The hell realms didn't spare him just because of his youth. It was chaos and anger and mean and cruel.

His floating turned to desperate swimming, then running on dead legs. The blue was his refuge. He was coming back for more, with or without an angel.

Pity that.

—

The spinning never stopped: a fleeting passage of light that rose in the east and set in the west. Rose in the north, sunk in the south. Came up from below, and disappeared back down again. A yelling first breath and a gasping last. All the while, floating, life spun on the invisible axis, some sort of cosmic order that, once enlarged, never made any sense. Where is the centre of the universe? What question has no answer? Is the mind the tool to know, or the intellect, or the heart?

At times more erect, Man staggered upright, engorged, impassioned and aflame, only to fall flaccid and spent – again and again and again. Crawled back for more.

Woman held out her arms in hopeful embrace, other times swept them up in forceful nurture and powered on with her feet firmly planted in the soil. Only later to be pulled back down too, by the moon and the movement of tides. None of them were free of each other, nor should they have been as they mixed their breath with every breath of Caesar and Buddha, Christ, Helene and Hecate. The oldest mother was not a nun and her mating was visceral, terrifying. Tara was radiant in ecstasy. The New Age collected the detritus of wisdoms left by the tsunami of greed and ignorance. It's too easy to wish on shooting stars, even to collect meteorites (or is that memories?) on the frozen lands where they are shuffled together against the mountains by receding ice; they're a dime a dozen. To really know takes time: a diamond moment. It's the age of carbon.

Even in a rock you can see the numinous.

⌒

The narrative wasn't spelt out. Too many struggled to find out where they were going; too few knew where they were. The poem broke through. It sounded like that single bell tolling, like that primordial Om, the cry of a baby's first breath. He remembered being lost in ecstasy, lying inside her body, nothing left to shed and the separation dissolved. The light burst through their tears of joy and suffering; release and oblivion. Another time, the same feeling, watching platypus on a farm dam. They both swam blind beneath the water. Each time, dissolved, he lost himself. Who was he? 'I am That' a long forgotten sacred text extolled, but he'd already put down the books.

～

Most were swept up and thrown forth again, all except Pete. He and Stonehouse burnt the final fuse. Perhaps you too have met someone incandescent – luminous is truer – jogging down the track with nimble feet and old hands. Can you see the Zen Master's breath, given out with joyous expulsion and the lightest of intake? See the smile as plumes of dust rise up from his soles. We never see him die; but I bet he does in peace. Or maybe he never will. Among us the saints still glide and the sacred is still to be beheld in a single flower. I saw a sassafras seed sprout in a forest full of bracken fronds. I've always loved weeds growing from pavement cracks. The gods are gardeners – and you? It doesn't really matter if we harvest, as long as we tend the saplings with loving lassitude and laughter and let them go. There is enough fruit for us all; so many have written that.

The platitudes are plentiful and silence rings sublime. The pen dries, the blood thins. Time to compost the creator, cremate the creation, pour the ash out into the ocean; let the fish swallow it up. Far better than storing it up in a mantelpiece urn, or bookshelf, for some later action or the next time round. Oceans deep, true blue, love of a kind immortal, there when the flesh has turned to ash: or fishmeal.

Renunciation is just gardening with our souls.

～

Bill bet on a full house. Poker was the game. It was all he ever had to go on: a full house, three over pair. When he was forced to leave by the king of hearts, he only had the brothers to behold.

But of the three of them Mick was already estranged, scarred by other fights, and Johnny was too young to call on. Still the cards were similarly dealt. Now that's baggage!

Mick was trying for the royal flush. John was aiming for the joker – he wanted the freedom of all possibilities. The youngest always did; born to rebel, the pattern goes. This game held another choice. They were ageless; their memory was as open as an abandoned hut, its door swinging on broken hinges. It is hard to draw a line between the inside and the out. They could, in just this briefest of moments, play it all wild. The pack was full of jokers.

So why did Mick keep trying to hold onto the king of diamonds?

But it's not Mick's and John's story now; they've had their say.

Billy grinned and looked at his cards.

—

'Play the bloody card, Corporal.'

It was before he lost his legs, his life. Wasn't it?

They were so low, three fives, hang ten plus one. China Beach felt cool on his mind. A wild time. Ditch the ace – too lonely. Learning to surf in Vietnam ended up being a career highlight. It was like dancing.

'Woo-hoo. Who's the big player now?' The GI was a wanker – an oldest child for sure – he gloated over the discarded ace.

'Shut up, Johnson. Your turn.'

'Keep your knickers on, girls. You're gonna lose.'

Johnson swung his beer can in a sweep around the table, knocked his helmet to the ground where it rolled headless into the corner. He laid down the queen of hearts, almost held a straight. 'Fuck me I'm hot!' he yelled.

The sergeant discarded the five of hearts.

Bill was silent as he picked it up and laid down five of a kind. This time he held the joker. The stumps where his legs should have been didn't feel like they looked. He danced with joy. How many legs do you need to surf in the *bardo*, the in-between?

It couldn't have happened like this; the nurses must have held him down screaming as they shot him full of morphine. He didn't attend the end. If he had, he might have got free.

⌣

The old man lay dying in solitude. In the hospice room, full of people and machines, his final moments were alone. In his ears the sounds of the monitors had ceased and his wheezing breath was only a whisper. Dying felt like eternity, a slow unravelling of time into oblivion. He was anxious but not afraid. Death had been coming for so long and every day he'd sat there at that bush bus stop, he'd been watching it coming: and going.

In the bed he held the photograph of his boys with easy hands and caressed each face in turn till his hands ceased to move of his accord and lay at random rest. His eyes closed and his sight looked distant; still he could see out the window that looked west towards the setting sun, towards the mountains covered in trees and the bush where he'd sat for twenty years of quiet communion.

When the lines went flat and the beep remained unbroken, the warmth of his body retreated to his heart and left a current coursing out of the top of his head. Around him the nurses quietened the machines, unplugged the cords and cables and drew the covers over his body. They made the calls, and old Frank senior was no more.

The light was luminous on the final day,
when the children of the underworld were set aflame,
and gripping the wheel one more time,
they turned it once again.

Moulting Lagoon

There is truth, there is story, there is the mind's fine line.

THERE IS A PAINTING BY the colonial artist John Glover of Moulting Lagoon on the east coast of Tasmania. Glover painted the scenery in 1838 after the Black War had ended and the remaining Aboriginal people who could be found had been taken off their lands to Flinders Island in the Bass Strait. The oil painting shows an Elysian view of the landscape. In the distance the pink granite hills of the Hazards on Freycinet Peninsula offer an appealing backdrop to the wide flat grazing lands in the middle ground where sheep fatten. The waterways of Great Oyster Bay and Moulting Lagoon thread neatly to one side, shining in the light. They show a clear blue expansiveness mirroring an open sky that takes up half the painting. On a hill in the foreground stands a convict stockman in a red coat, gazing out over his flock, with his attentive dog.

There is no fear in the painting, no telltale plumes of smoke from burning huts or raided campsites. No worrying wildness, no hinted-at sounds of screaming. All is silent and peaceful. Glover has tidied and reduced the wetlands that the land commissioners for Van Diemen's Land (as they called it then) a few years earlier called 'the largest swamp... in the Colony'. As the scholar David Hansen notes: 'Artists of Glover's generation would often edit or enhance the visible world, correcting nature's compositional untidinesses in accordance with the conventions of classical landscape.' It is a style now called 'the colonial picturesque'.

Not everybody saw it this way. Yes, Glover's imagery was described by the *Colonial Times* in glowing terms: 'These pictures will convey a more correct idea than the mere reading of books of travel can convey... the country itself is beautiful and picturesque... in some districts magnificent and sublime.' But the wife of the governor of Van Diemen's land, Lady Jane Franklin, was not so enamoured: 'If his pictures there are no better than those I saw exhibited of his in London before our departure, they are not worth much.'

—

In 1830 a short spear was pulled from the body of a ploughman on Apsley, the grazing property of the colonist William Lyne. This is the same property in Glover's scene: Lyne having been 'granted' this land in 1826. Glover painted the scene from Pine Hill which was, according to the journal of the land commissioners, 'a long narrow slip of upland... the most heavily timbered and worst part of his [Lyne's] farm. He cleared it at heavy expence [sic]'. Conflict with the local inhabitants led to Lyne constructing at least one fortified hut on Apsley.

In response to the killings of colonists, retribution on the Aboriginal people who had lived on their land, Lutruwita, for millennia, was swift. Dozens were killed, women and children included. It was only one of many incidences in the Black War that raged across the land for nearly thirty years from 1804 to 1832.

—

Moulting Lagoon is now a Ramsar site, a sanctuary for wildlife and a favourite campground for east coast holidaymakers. *Allocasuarinas*, or she-oaks, offer up a carpet of soft needles on sandy grounds on which to pitch a tent. They provide a sheltered shoreline to watch wild ducks and swans fly in during evening.

In March, during the hunting season, the ducks continue to fly in from the south to shelter in the shallow waters. They pass over the thatched tea-tree hides of hunters just south of the main lagoon. It must be like flying into a war zone.

—

Haley and Freddy were camping at Moulting Lagoon. In their car was a pile of small, blackened boulders taken from the ruins of John's hut and they were scattering them around the island at places they knew John loved. It was their requiem, Haley had quietly insisted. Freddy's language had regressed since John died but Haley saw the way he fiercely hung onto the rocks he had gathered from Grey Mountain. They were an unlikely life raft in the wordless ocean that swelled within him, and she negotiated the camping trip as a way of getting him to release them – and maybe find his words again.

At each campground Freddy built small fireplaces with the

stones, and Haley listened as he sang his mournful dirges in sounds only he could understand. The first night at Moulting Lagoon he poked the fire with a stick and flayed at the sparks that rose. Haley intoned in the background, a quiet moan – almost a wail – as the tears rolled down her face. The strange harmony of their voices dispersed into the bush without echo. The night air was quiet, with only the gentle lapping of water among the reeds. Freddy's incantations rose and fell but eventually they ceased, and both he and Haley stared vacantly at the fire's dimming embers.

Later, exhausted, they lay out in the open with their sleeping bags close and gazed at the clear night sky. The Aurora pulsed and in the curtains of flowing white light Freddy heard other rhythms. He remembered his Grunkle Jack's poems, not as words, but as feelings. His breathing steadied and he fell asleep.

—

Just before dusk on the second night at Moulting Lagoon, three carloads of men turned up with spotlights blazing and enough camping equipment to last a lifetime. They set up on the lagoon edge, just along from Haley and Freddy, corralling the cars and firing up a generator for the fridges, lights and radios. Freddy watched, puzzled and inquisitive, and Haley tried to explain what they were doing. Hunting wasn't something foreign to him, he'd watched his great-uncle Jack kill wallaby for food up on Grey Mountain, but something about the scale of this sudden invasion scared him; something more than simply the contrast to their night before. As they lay in the tent that night listening to the loud voices and music, he kept tossing about and making distressed sounds and it was a long time before Haley felt him settle.

They were woken by the sounds of gunshots. Volleys of dull thuds brought Freddy upright and shivering in the pre-dawn air. Outside the tent, the light among the she-oaks was only just enough to make out the shapes of the trees. Through them, out into the lagoon, the water and sky were gunmetal grey. The shooting continued.

Freddy was up and out of the tent before Haley could stop him. He ran through the trees down to the water's edge and stood ankle deep between the reeds, staring out at the wicker hides from where the sounds of shots carried over the water. As the sky lightened and he looked across the bay to the southeast, he could see ducks in broken formations circling and flying low towards the safety of more distant wetlands. But still other birds came on above the hides, and the firing continued. Freddy saw the sudden holes in the sky as the birds fell, raining down into the swamp like cold stones. Other shapes were wading out from the hides across the shallows. As the dawn came on the silhouettes of hanging birds could be seen thumping against the hunters' shoulders.

When Haley joined Freddy by the water's edge and placed a rug around his slumped shoulders he turned and looked at her, and she saw in his eyes the full weight of his sadness. Her voice was raspy in the cold air, her breath foggy.

'We'll go into the mountains today,' she said. 'Up to Cradle, camp at Peggy's place. Light another fire there.'

Freddy shook his head vigorously.

'Stay,' he said.

It was the first word Haley could fathom since John's death. It was her turn to shake her head.

'But they'll be hunting tomorrow too.'

She tried to pull him close but Freddy shook her off, turned and splashed back through the trampled muddy reeds to their campsite.

—

All that day Freddy wandered the vagrant edge of the wetland, weaving in and out of the shallows in sandshoes blackened by the mud. Haley followed at a distance, respecting his need for solitude, worried about his mood. The first time she saw him sink to his knees and bury his arms into the water she thought he'd stumbled on the tea tree roots and rotting clumps of *Juncus* reeds but when she got to him, she saw he was cradling something in his arms. His head was bowed and he was whispering gentle sounds. It was a bird, one the hunters hadn't collected, the lifeless wings sodden and dulled. Freddy stroked the lolling bottle-green head; the teal's lifeless eyes stared impassively in return. He carried it away from the water's edge and dug a shallow grave in the sandy soil. Then he trudged all the way back to the campsite and returned with a single stone that he placed on the grave. All the while he ignored Haley, shrugging off her attempts to comfort him but not trying to hide from her. She followed at a distance, her breath catching, her chest tight.

Freddy walked the lagoon edge all day, searching among the reeds. By the time he found the fifth bird it was getting near dusk. This time the bird had managed to drag itself out of the water and into a thicket of tussocks. Freddy saw a trail of blood on the ground and traced it into the clump, pushing aside the tangled leaves with sudden haste. But the bird lay on its side, its chestnut breast feathers matted with coagulated blood, its pale blue, dished bill pushed partly under an outstretched wing. He again sank to his knees, reached out and gently straightened the displaced feathers, moved the head to a more comfortable position.

Haley looked at her son; it was time to go back to the campsite. He was starting to shiver, the chill from his wet clothes finally registering on his skin, and she too was trembling. She held out her hands and this time he picked up the dead bird and gave it to her, letting her carry it back towards the campground. Just before they got there they cleared a spot under the Oyster Bay pines and dug the grave together. When Haley asked him if he wanted to get another of John's stones, he shook his head and instead placed a close-by piece of mudstone on top of the mound.

That night a light rain saw them cook with the gas stove and the fireplace remained cold. They sheltered in the tent and Haley told Freddy stories of John's early life. Stories she'd heard from John in their long rambling raves when she lived nearby and used to drop into his old suburban house. Some of the stories Freddy knew, and he smiled at the familiar tones and a warmth spread over his body. Haley felt his rocking quieten and they both fell asleep to the drumming of the rain on the tent, which muted the noise of the other campers.

—

What woke Haley the next morning was both familiar and misplaced. At first she thought she was still dreaming; the mournful, sonorous call of the radong radiating into her awareness from mountain echoes and shack visits. But the rustle of her sleeping bag and the emptiness of the mat beside her brought her up sharp. It was still dark as she quickly unzipped the tent and followed the sound to the water's edge. Cloud masked the dawn, but angry voices carried across the water between the trumpet blasts. Freddy was standing somewhere out there amidst the hides, blowing relentlessly. Splashes and threatening voices moved towards him, and she hurried after the sounds.

'Don't hurt him,' she yelled into the darkness.

'Like fuck we won't lady,' came a reply. 'We'll silence the prick. Where the fuck is he?'

Freddy was moving about, trumpeting irregularly now, hiding among the hides. The ducks were wheeling and honking further away. The splashing of the hunters was chaotic as they waded about trying to get a fix on the trumpet sound. Gunshots boomed.

The sky continued to lighten and the telltale V's of the flying birds remained distant as they arced around the hides and safely landed further up the lagoon. As Freddy came closer to the shore the hunters caught up with him. Four of them surrounded him, blocking Haley's vision as she thrashed towards them through the water. Their torches flashed saber-like, their guns pointed threateningly. The pockets on their hunting vests bulged with unspent ammunition.

'What the fuck are you doing, mate?'

'Who do you think you are? You got shit-for-brains or what?'

'We've a licence to be here – and you're really pissing us off.'

'You'll regret that little game – I don't give a fuck who else is here.'

They shoved him, pushing him hard against each other. One

grabbed at the long flute of the radong, trying to wrench it from Freddy. Another punched him in the back. Haley finally caught up with them and threw herself against the nearest hunter.

'He's only a boy, leave him,' she yelled.

'Old enough to fuck'n know better. Cunt.' The hunter swivelled on her and slapped her away and she stumbled onto her knees in the water.

'Look at him, you bastards. Just look at him!' she screamed.

Two torch beams pointed at Freddy's face, and what the light revealed suddenly stilled them all. His eyes stared straight back at them, the black of his pupils shining, the whites mottled. Sloping hooded eyelids flowed smooth from the low bridge of his nose. His round face was chillingly serene. They looked at the distinctive features of the Down syndrome boy and felt a flood of shame.

'Grunkle Jack's flying there,' he said in a quiet voice full of power.

He stared at each of them in turn, holding each man with his unblinking gaze. Then he pushed through them, turned towards the breaking sunrise, and strode like a warrior to the shore.

Acknowledgements

The author gratefully acknowledges Aki Matsusa for her English translation of Basho's famous haiku written in Japanese around 1691. Heartfelt thanks also go to Stephenie Cahalan and Veronica McShane for early edits on the manuscript; to Julia Gibson for patient re-readings, support and keeping the home fires burning; and to Danielle Wood and fellow writers from the 2013 University of Tasmania MA Creative writing group for the first weeding of the garden. Much gratitude to Sue Young and Ashwood Publishing for careful final edits and carrying this book to completion.

About the Author

Andy 'Ryugen' Baird has lived in Lutruwita / Tasmania for the last 35 years, drawn to the island as a sacred land of possibility, existential homecoming and deep natural beauty. He spent his early working life in environmental education, with time in high schools, outdoors in Landcare and Bushcare roles, and in places as diverse as Antarctica, the Arctic and as an environmental trainer in the Dalai Lama's monastery in India. He also worked for many years at the Tasmanian Museum and Art Gallery. In 2021 he ordained as a Zen Buddhist monk and now resides in a straw-stone-timber home and hermitage he built with his partner in the Huon Valley, sitting amongst the trees and offering up whatever love, peace and beauty he can manifest through his writings. He also chops wood!

9 781764 125444